"What did you think of church?" Larissa asked, expectantly.

"I thought you were the most beautiful woman there."

"That's not what I asked.

They drove along in silence for a while. She thought Drew was asleep behind his sunglasses until out of the blue, he said, "I liked your church."

Her mouth curved in a smile. "Does that mean you'll go again some time?"

"Larissa."

And just like that the sun went behind a cloud.

"I've always wanted you beside me at church. I loved having you there."

She sounded pitiful, begging him.

Drew removed the sunglasses. "If it's that important to you."

Hope bloomed, sweet and lovely. God was at work. She had to keep believing.

Books by Linda Goodnight

Love Inspired

LINDA GOODNIGHT

A romantic at heart, Linda Goodnight believes in the traditional values of family and home. Writing books enables her to share her belief that, with faith and perseverance, love can last forever and happy endings really are possible.

A native of Oklahoma, Linda lives in the country with her husband, Gene, and Mugsy, an adorably obnoxious rat terrier. She and Gene have a blended family of six grown children. An elementary school teacher, she is also a licensed nurse. When time permits, Linda loves to read, watch football and rodeo, and indulge in chocolate. She also enjoys taking long, calorie-burning walks in the nearby woods. Readers can write to her at linda@lindagoodnight.com, or c/o Steeple Hill Books, 233 Broadway, Suite 1001, New York, NY 10279.

The Heart of Grace
Linda Goodnight

Steeple
Hill®

Published by Steeple Hill Books™

STEEPLE HILL BOOKS

Steeple
Hill®

ISBN-13: 978-0-373-81315-5
ISBN-10:   0-373-81315-5

THE HEART OF GRACE

Printed in U.S.A.

Though you have made me see troubles, many and bitter, you will restore my life again; from the depths of the earth you will again bring me up.

—*Psalms* 71:20

To Gene, with all my love.

Prologue

Drew Grace jerked away from the office door and whirled, poised to run. A social worker was in there. He knew what that meant. It meant trouble.

Heart pounding, he pushed at the teacher blocking his way. A pair of strong hands, those of the school counselor, Mr. James, caught his shoulders and forced him inside the long narrow office.

Fury ripped through Drew, hot and powerful. He doubled up his fist. He might be only seven but he was tough and he could fight. He wasn't ever scared to fight no matter how big the other guy. Anybody that didn't believe that could ask Timothy Wilson. Timothy was in fourth grade but Drew bloodied his nose and made him cry yesterday on the playground. Stupid idiot said

Drew stunk. So maybe he did. Big deal. It wasn't none of Timothy's business anyway.

"Sit down, Drew," Mr. James said. "We need to talk to you boys about something."

Talk. Yeah, sure. Drew knew better. They weren't going to talk. They were going to drag him and his brothers off to foster care again.

He wasn't going. Foster parents never liked him. They were mean. They said he was a troublemaker.

Well, he didn't like them either. If grown-ups would just leave them alone, they'd be okay. Or if Mama would come home. When she was in the chips she brought them presents. That's what she said, in the chips.

His heart hurt a little to think of Mama. And that just made him madder. He slammed the clenched fist into the social worker's gut and pushed past her. Mr. James grabbed him around the waist. Kicking, flailing with all his might, Drew growled like a mad dog as the counselor pushed him into a chair.

Drew gazed frantically around the room looking for escape. He had to get out of here.

His big brother Collin stood beside the counselor's desk, face as cold and hard as ice, arms tight at his sides. Drew knew that look. Collin was mad and probably scared, too, though he always said he wasn't.

His baby brother Ian sat in a chair at the end of the room. Silent tears made dirty streaks on his face. Poor little kid. He was always nice to everybody. He was still in pre-K so what did he know. Ian didn't yet understand all the things that Drew and Collin did. Sometimes you couldn't be nice.

Drew tried to take care of Ian 'cause he was so little. Well, Drew and Collin together. Collin always knew the best places to find food and stuff.

They had a hiding place, a good one. If he could just get out of here, he'd head there. Maybe the teachers would chase him and give Collin and Ian a chance to escape, too. He was fast. He could outrun them. Then he'd be the hero, and his brothers would give him the biggest share of food. They'd make a fire and build a fort. Just him and his brothers against the world. They could do it.

Sometimes Collin got them out of trouble. But not always. Drew knew he couldn't count on anything when adults were involved. He and Ian and Collin could make it okay by themselves. They always had.

Drew knew how to make a fire. He liked fire.

He liked to watch the flames lick up the side of paper and turn it bright orange. He liked the smell of matches.

Just then some nosy teacher walked by and stuck her fat head inside the office. Behind glasses, her eyes bugged out.

"Poor little things," he heard her whisper right before the social worker shut the door in her face. "Living in that old burned-out trailer, that trashy mother gone half the time. No wonder they're filthy."

Drew exploded out of the chair and started toward the door. He'd make her pay for saying that.

But once again, Mr. James caught him. This time he wasn't too gentle. He pushed Drew down into the plastic chair and held him there. Most times Drew liked Mr. James okay, but not today.

"Collin," the social worker said to his big brother. She had a hand on her belly where Drew had punched her. He didn't care. She shouldn't be sticking her nose into his business. That's what Mama said. If welfare would just keep their nose out of her business, everything would be fine. "You've been through this before. You know it's for the best. Why don't you help us get your brothers in the car?"

Collin ignored her. Drew figured his brother was thinking the same thing he was. They had to get out of here.

Ian started sniveling, making hiccuping sounds like he was trying to keep from crying. Drew wanted to go to him and say everything would be okay. But he'd be lying. He didn't want to lie to his brother. Besides, Mr. James was holding him down like a wrestler and wouldn't let him up.

Collin must have noticed Ian, too, because he walked right past that social worker like he didn't even see her and laid a hand on Ian's head. Ian looked up at Collin with wet blue eyes and stopped crying. He kind of shivered like a cold kitten, and Drew got mad all over again. A little kid like that shouldn't have to be scared all the time.

The social worker must have noticed Ian crying, too, because she knelt in front of his chair and told some big lie about taking them to a nice house and buying them all new shoes. Poor kid believed every word. Drew wished it was true, but it wasn't.

Mr. James, who smelled like spearmint gum, loosened his hold the slightest bit and slid to his knees in front of Drew's chair. Drew hoped this was his chance. Mr. James, who coached baseball and was stronger than some of the high school football players, wasn't a dummy. He kept one big hand on Drew's arm and another on his knee.

"Boys," he said, looking around at all three of them. "Sometimes life throws us a curveball. Things happen that we don't expect. But I want you to know one thing." He stared over at the social worker. She was still on her knees in front of Ian. "No matter where you go from here or what happens, you have a friend who will never leave you. His name is Jesus. If you let Him, He'll take care of you."

Something inside Drew quieted. He knew who Jesus was though he'd never been to church. He didn't know how he knew but he did. And even if it was a lie, he liked thinking that there was somebody somewhere that wouldn't leave him and his brothers alone.

"Collin?" Mr. James said and twisted around, holding his hand out. When Collin ignored him, the counselor laid the hand on Collin's worn-out shoe and bowed his head. He started whispering something and Drew knew Mr. James was praying. Praying for Collin and Ian and him.

Drew got a funny lump in his chest, like he

might cry. He squeezed his eyes shut. Mr. James loosened his hold, but Drew didn't try to run. He wasn't mad at Mr. James, not really. He wanted Mr. James to take him home with him and teach him how to play baseball.

When the prayer was over, Drew opened his eyes, curious. The room was real quiet. Even Ian had stopped whimpering.

Mr. James reached into his pocket and pulled out some little key chains and handed them each one. Drew gazed at his, curious about the silver metal fish with words on the back.

He was in second grade. He could read. But not that good.

"I want you to have one of these," the counselor said. He stared at the social worker again in a way Drew didn't understand, like he was daring her to say anything. She looked down and fiddled with the floppy sole of Ian's shoe. "It's a reminder of what I said, that God will watch over you no matter where you go or what you do."

"Where we going this time?" Collin asked, voice hard and mad.

"I have placements for Drew and Ian."

"Together?"

Drew's head jerked up. They always stayed together. They had to stay together.

"Not this time. All the placements are separate."

Blood pounded in Drew's head. He clenched the key chain until the metal bit into his skin.

"Ian gets scared," Collin said, his voice shaky. "He stays with me."

Collin was right. Ian needed his big brothers. They needed each other. All for one, one for all. Like the Three Musketeers movie they saw at a friend's house.

Drew's blood started to heat up again. Separate placements. Places for bad boys. For troublemakers.

He looked frantically at Collin. Why didn't Collin say something? Why didn't he tell her that they couldn't be separated? They'd die if they weren't together.

He opened his mouth to say so, but only a growl came out.

"I'm sorry, boys. This will work out for the best. You'll see." The social worker tried to sound jolly, but Drew was no fool.

They would be separated. Him and Collin and Ian. He would never see his brothers again.

He said a cussword and bolted toward the door. Too late, too late. Mr. James picked him up and carried him out the door, kicking and screaming.

Chapter One

~

Twenty-three years later, Iraq

Life as he knew it was about to end.

Drew Michaels had made a mistake and now he had to pay the price. No matter how much it hurt, no matter how badly he wanted to hang on, he had to let go of the most important thing in his life—his marriage.

He just hoped he could survive the aftermath.

"Mr. Michaels, take a shot of that."

Camera ever ready, Drew followed the direction of his driver's pointed finger but didn't press the shutter. He was on assignment somewhere outside Baghdad, and if he'd seen one herd of goats he'd seen them all. He wasn't in much of a mood today to take useless photos.

Or any kind of photos, come to think of it. The memory of yesterday's telephone conversation with Larissa was too fresh and painful.

He'd finally told her the truth.

Well, not the real truth, but the truth she needed to hear. Their marriage had been a mistake, and he wanted a divorce.

Remembering her reaction made him want to shoot something all right, but not with his camera.

Larissa had cried. He hated himself for that, just as he hated himself for ever thinking he could make a woman like her happy. Any woman, for that matter. Drew Michaels didn't have what it took to settle down and be a husband and father. He wanted to. He just couldn't.

He and Amil, the amiable Iraqi driver, were bumping through another nameless village with the usual string of squat, sand-colored buildings and local citizens going about the normal business of living. Women in long, flowing *abayahs,* children herding goats with a stick, soldiers poised with automatic rifles.

Drew had spent so much time in the Middle East that the military presence had actually started to look normal to him.

Next week he was off to Indonesia. A volcano was on the howl, and disasters were his specialty. Earthquakes, volcanoes, famine, war. You name it, he shot it. Not the usual stuff though. That was boring. He either went for that elusive moment of ambient light or for the people, the human side, the kids. He was good and he knew it. In fact, photography was the only thing he'd ever been good at. If he'd stuck to his work, he wouldn't be in this mess now.

Sand swirled up in front of the jeep and Drew shaded his face. Sunglasses weren't adequate protection against Middle Eastern sand and a photographer couldn't be too careful of his eyes.

Photographic art buffs said he had great artistic vision, an eye for the perfect detail. Able to capture an image that spoke to the consciousness.

He didn't know about all that, but he didn't argue. If they wanted to pay exorbitant prices for his photos, he'd take their money.

The memory of one particular photo exhibition shimmied to the surface. Tulsa. Three years ago.

He'd felt as phony as his last name. All those society types swarming around a display of his work, murmuring things like, "inspired," or "provocative."

He should have known then to cut and run. But he hadn't.

And then Larissa had walked toward him, an

artsy diamond choker around her elegant neck, sparkling diamonds dangling from her ears. His eye for detail had served him well at that moment, though he'd wished for a camera to capture her. In a long white fitted gown of some satiny material, chestnut hair pulled up at the sides, one gleaming lock over a bare shoulder, she'd captivated him.

He'd never expected to love anybody, but he'd fallen in love with Larissa on the spot. It was stupid and foolish. Now he had to right the wrong he'd done to her.

"Another week and I'm out of here, Amil," he said to the driver.

"Going home to your woman, huh?"

His woman. The words poked at him like a sticker. He should have known back then that Larissa was too wonderful for a street bum like him. He should have known he didn't have what it took to be a husband.

Attention diverted by a soldier and an Iraqi toddler in a pink dress, Drew didn't bother to answer. Some things hurt too much to discuss.

A G.I., gun slung behind him, had gone down on both knees to tie a little girl's shoe. The contrast was stunning—an innocent toddler and a hardened marine gentled by a child's trust.

Drew pressed the shutter. Now *that* was a picture.

In front of them, two other jeeps bounced along. Though he normally worked alone, he'd been lucky to tag along on this trek into the countryside. They had a meeting with one of the tribal chiefs, and a man never knew what might come of that.

His vest rattled with rolls of film and various lenses as he reached into his inner pocket and removed a photo of Larissa. He'd taken hundreds of the woman who was his wife. She was a photographer's dream, all grace and class and innocence.

He clenched his teeth. His wife. The burning ache in his gut grew hotter. Must be getting an ulcer, a common malady for a disaster photographer.

Larissa was his love, his life, and his wife. But in three years he'd never been the man she needed. The phone call yesterday had been the hardest call he'd ever made. He hadn't slept more than three hours all week, working up to that call.

Tulsa with Larissa was the only home he'd ever known, but now that was gone, too. He couldn't go back and face her. If he did, he might chicken out. For her sake, he'd remain abroad. And selfish as always, he'd lose himself in the job and leave the dirty work to his lawyer.

His chest pinched tight as he thought of all the things she wanted that he couldn't give her. Himself mostly, but lately she'd mentioned babies.

Even though the temperature outside hovered somewhere around a hundred and ten degrees, Drew shivered. Babies. The idea scared him more than walking through a minefield. Larissa didn't know, didn't understand the dark, secret reasons why he could never, ever father a child.

"She is very beautiful."

"What?" Drew glanced over at Amil. "Oh, Larissa. My wife." The words fell from his lips as if he needed to call her his as long as he could.

"You are a lucky man."

"She wants a baby," he blurted and then wondered why. It was a moot point now.

"So give her one. A fine son to carry on your name."

Which name? he wondered grimly. Michaels? Grace? Another of the reasons he had to let her go. Larissa had no clue she'd married a man who didn't exist. Wouldn't that be a shocker to her rich, politician daddy?

He'd done all right as Drew Michaels,

though, and had gained a bit of a reputation with his work. Even if he did feel like a fraud most of the time, he was fine as long as no one else discovered the truth. But he wouldn't pass that legacy of lies on to an innocent child. He knew what happened to kids who came from bad bloodlines.

After making sure Amil's attention had returned to the convoy in front of them, Drew touched the photo to his lips, then slid it back into his vest. Over his heart. She *was* his heart and always would be, long after the ink was dried on the divorce papers, and she was happily married to some nice man who could give her all the babies she wanted.

"You come to Amil's house," the driver was saying. "I will show you sons. Seven of them, I have. They will make you smile and you can—" He lifted one hand from the steering wheel and pretended to snap pictures.

Drew was readying a wisecrack when suddenly, the world exploded.

In a split second of horror, he comprehended the sound and knew what was happening.

Attack. A roadside bomb. God help them all.

The last thing his conscious mind registered was the smile fading from Amil's face and the bizarre experience of flying backward out of the jeep, one hand frantically gripping his Nikon.

He screamed Larissa's name.

Larissa Stone Michaels sat straight up in bed, heart thundering louder than an Oklahoma rainstorm.

Another bad dream. The third time this week she'd awakened from a terrible nightmare that she couldn't remember. Any time Drew was in the Middle East, she suffered sleepless nights and bad dreams.

Then the memory of yesterday's phone conversation flooded into her consciousness. No wonder she'd had another nightmare. Drew wanted a divorce.

A sob choked out, loud in the silent bedroom. The little Yorkie, Coco, lying at the foot of the bed, raised her tiny head. Larissa pressed a hand to quivering lips, holding back the sorrow that had ended only when she'd finally fallen asleep.

She glanced at the illuminated clock on the curio lamp stand. Four in the morning. Less than three hours since she'd last noted the time.

Many nights she awakened unable to sleep until she'd prayed for Drew's safety. But this night was different. This night, she didn't have that sweet promise that her husband loved her and would be coming home to her.

He was never coming home again.

Tossing back the duvet comforter, she swung both feet to the plush carpet. Her body trembled. The soft whoosh of the heating unit was the only sound in the quiet Southside villa. Weary and heartsick, she went into the bathroom and flicked on the light. After a moment of blindness she found a glass, ran it full of water and drank deeply. The reflection in the mirror looked wild, dark hair tangled around a pale face.

"Oh, Drew," she whispered to the mirror. "What did I do? What happened?"

With grim determination, she swallowed hard against the ache in her throat, pushing back the tears. She couldn't keep doing this. She had to get hold of her emotions long enough to think things through.

She'd had no idea anything was wrong until the phone call. She loved him. Six months ago when he was home, everything had been as good as ever. Before he left for Iraq, he'd held her such a long time and told her how much he loved and needed her.

And now this.

"Jesus. Dear Jesus."

Hands braced on the sink, she squeezed her eyes tight and did the only thing she knew to do. She prayed. For Drew's safety, first and always. For their bewilderingly troubled marriage. For her breaking heart.

But this time the usual sense of peace evaded her. Her emotions were too raw and confused.

She returned to the bedroom, certain she'd slept her last. As she slipped beneath the petal-soft sheets, the phone rang.

A frightful pounding in her temples started up. A call at this time of night could not be good news.

She picked up the receiver and said, "Hello?"

And the nightmare began again. Only this time, she was awake.

Chapter Two

Drew hurt everywhere. His head, his leg, his back, his guts. Even his hair hurt.

He tried to open his eyes but they were too heavy. The drugs, he supposed. Drugs were good, but they didn't eliminate the pain. They only made him stupid, too groggy to form an intelligent sentence, too relaxed to care.

The first time he'd awakened after the blast, he'd been in a helicopter. The whump, whump, whump had sent him into violent tremors. Shock, the docs in Germany said.

Well yes, he was shocked. Getting blown up wasn't on his list of fun things to do.

He wondered where his cameras were.

"Mr. Michaels." A male voice penetrated the haze. Someone lifted his wrist and felt his pulse. Hard, strong fingers. He wanted the voice to go away but figured he'd slept his allotted quota for the day.

Around this place fifteen minutes was tops before someone else came along to poke, prod or wheel him off to radiology. He'd been scanned and x-rayed so much he probably glowed in the dark. A radioactive photographer.

Funny. He had a brief image of using the glow from his body as available light to snap photos. All good photographers experimented with different light sources. And he was good. Really good. Everybody said so. Especially Larissa. She thought he was wonderful.

Larissa. The sharpest pain yet hit him.

Did she know how much he loved her? Did she know he was hurt? He hoped not. She'd be upset. He'd already caused her enough trouble.

The floaty feeling came back and he leaned into it, ready to go where it led. Thinking of Larissa hurt too much to remain conscious.

"Mr. Michaels."

With an inner sigh, Drew resurfaced and managed to raise his eyelids. Squinting at the bright light and too-white room, he saw his tormenter. A doctor. But he wasn't sure which one. That was one of the problems he'd been having.

His memory wasn't as good as it used to be. Things were a little fuzzy. His head hurt. A lot.

"I've never been in a hospital," he grumbled.

"So you told me."

He had?

Eyes wider now, he focused on the physician's name badge. Dr. Pascal. Neurology. "When can I get out of here?"

The doctor sidestepped the question with one of his own. "How's the vision? Any more problems?"

Drew's gut lurched. He didn't like thinking about the hours of blackness that had surrounded him after the blast. "Twenty-twenty."

"Let's have a look."

Drew wondered who *let's* was. Doctors all seemed to speak as if they were polymorphic. The God complex, he supposed.

His own drug-twisted humor amused him, but in truth, if he looked at the doc too long, he saw more than one. He sobered instantly. There was nothing funny about that.

Two were better than none, but still…

Dr. Pascal's thick fingers stretched Drew's eyelids apart while shining a pin light back and forth. Back and forth. The doc smelled like mouthwash and antiseptic soap.

"No more episodes of blindness? Double vision? Blurriness?"

"Some," he admitted, hating the truth but figuring the doc should know. "How long before it goes away for good?"

"No way to tell. You sustained a pretty nasty concussion, but the CAT scan didn't indicate anything permanent. If you're lucky, this will be gone by the time you are dismissed."

He'd only been lucky once in his life. The day he'd found Larissa. And look how that turned out.

If luck was required to heal his vision, he was in deep trouble.

The jitters in his belly turned to earthquakes. His eyes were everything. A photographer had to see and see clearly.

"Anything you can do for it?"

"Time." The doc fingered something on the bedside table. "And divine intervention, if you believe in such things."

Drew raised his pounding head ever so slightly and saw the doctor holding the small pewter fish he usually wore on a leather string around his neck. His hand went to his throat. He never liked to be without it. Someone had been thoughtful enough to realize that.

"I'm not a religious man."

He saw no point in explaining to the doc or anyone else that the ichthus was his only link to the past and to the brothers he hadn't seen in more than twenty years. Other than this small reminder, he had nothing. He didn't even know where they were.

Like Larissa, his brothers were gone.

Something deep inside him began to ache. He wished the morphine would kick in again.

The memory of his two brothers, of that last day in the school counselor's office sometimes overwhelmed him, especially when he was weak or sick or overtired.

Times like now. For a few painful seconds, Ian and Collin hovered on the edge of his mind.

Ian, cute and small and loving had probably been adopted. No one could resist that little dude. And Collin. Well, Collin was like him, a survivor. Collin would be okay.

Sometimes he wondered what it would be like to find them again, to be with his brothers, but he couldn't. Never would. He was no longer Drew Grace, pitiful child of a crack queen. He was Drew Michaels, successful photographer. He never wanted anyone, especially Larissa, to discover that he was literally nobody—a nobody with a deadly secret and a gutful of guilt.

Over the years, he'd become a master at forcing his brothers back into the box inside his mind where the past resided.

He did that now, carefully, painstakingly shutting the door on the childish faces of Ian and Collin Grace.

"The brain is an interesting organ," Dr. Pascal said, handing him the necklace without comment.

Drew reclaimed the ichthus, but didn't answer. He didn't know how interesting his brain was and didn't much care. But he couldn't afford to lose the one thing that made him a photographer—his eyes.

"Most visual disturbances resolve as the swelling in your brain returns to normal."

Drew swallowed. His throat was raw and scratchy from what the nurses called intubation. Basically, having a tube stuffed down his throat during surgery.

"And when the problems don't resolve themselves?" he asked.

The doctor patted his shoulder. "No use borrowing trouble. You have enough to think about."

Drew was not comforted. "What happens next?"

"In a few days your surgeons and I will look at dismissal. But you're still weak from the blood loss."

"Tell me about it." He could barely feed himself.

"Losing your spleen is a serious operation. How's the incision?"

"The other docs looked at it this morning. At least, I think it was this morning. They said it was looking good."

"You're fortunate to be healthy and in good physical shape. It probably saved your life."

"I'm a survivor," he said grimly.

"You'll need some rehab on the shattered ankle and heel and plenty of time for the broken ribs to mend."

"So, are you sending me to one of those rehab places?"

The doc's brown eyes crinkled as if he was about to offer Drew the grand prize. "Wouldn't you rather go home?"

The question was a kick in the gut. Sure, he'd like to go home. Wherever that was.

Larissa's knees trembled as she traversed the long white corridor toward Drew's hospital room. For five days, she'd done nothing but pray and make telephone calls and argue with her parents. Even though she was thirty-two years old, they still attempted to run her life. To their way of thinking, she never should have married Drew. And she sure shouldn't run to his bedside after he'd announced his intention to divorce her.

But how could she not? He was her husband and she loved him.

Right now, she refused to deal with the pressure from her parents. Knowing her husband was lying in a hospital bed, seriously injured was all she could handle. The list of injuries was frightening, to say the least. Broken ribs, ankle, heel, a ruptured spleen, and too many cuts and bruises for anyone to tell her about on the telephone. She was terrified to see him.

Her Prada heels echoed in the sterile white environment. She reached room 4723 and stopped, suddenly short of breath, not from the climb but from the uncertainty.

How would Drew look? Would he be conscious? Was he in awful pain?

The new worry crowded in. Would he want her here? Would he be angry that she had come after he'd made it clear that he never wanted to see her again?

During the time Drew was in a military hospital in Germany, she'd called every day. He either hadn't been able or willing to speak to her. Now that he was here in Walter Reed, she'd given up calling. She'd gotten on a plane and come.

The fact that he'd initiated a divorce didn't mean anything at this point. Drew was her husband. He needed her. And she was going to take care of him whether he liked it or not. During his recovery, she would pray every single day for God to change Drew's mind and heal their marriage. A politician's daughter didn't give up without a fight.

Fingers on the handle, she paused to draw in a steadying breath.

"Help me, Lord," she whispered, and then slowly pushed the heavy door inward.

The semi-darkened room was quiet. Drew was alone, eyes closed. A shiver of relief rippled through her. Though bruised and sutured, he still looked like Drew.

She breathed a prayer of gratitude. A roadside bomb often did much worse. From the bits and pieces of information she'd gathered, the rest of the convoy hadn't fared as well.

Given the rhythmic motion of his chest, Drew was sleeping. An IV machine *tick-ticked* at his bedside, and his left leg was elevated on pillows. A medicine scent permeated the small unit. Monitors she couldn't name crowded in around his bed. The whole scenario was surreal and frightening.

Heart in her throat, Larissa tiptoed inside, careful not to wake him. She wanted a minute to drink him in, to love him with her eyes, to remember all the beautiful times they'd had together. And most important of all, to thank God above that he remained alive and would recover. Her husband, her heart. How could he want to end the precious gift God had given them when they'd found each other?

As always, Drew looked larger than life, his tall form too big for the standard issue hospital bed, his skin dark against white sheets. One long, manly hand lay across his chest gripping the necklace he always wore. She'd asked him about the tiny fish more than once, but his vague answers hadn't satisfied. Now that she was a Christian, she wondered even more. Drew tolerated her new faith, but he wasn't interested in sharing it, which made his attachment to the necklace even more curious.

"A friend gave it to me when I was a kid," he'd say. "It's nothing special."

But she didn't believe that. Since he was never without it, she suspected the necklace carried a deeper meaning than he let on. But she had never pressed.

That was part of the problem in their marriage. She never pressed. Drew was dark and brooding at times and she'd learned to tiptoe around the topics that set him off. Part of the attraction from the beginning had been that air of mystery, the things he didn't say or talk about. She wanted to unlock the secrets and see inside his heart. She wanted to know him as he knew her. Drew had never allowed that. For a long time, she'd wondered if he'd ever let her in, if he'd ever let her know the real Drew Michaels. Now she knew he never would.

Once he'd mentioned a "tough" childhood and her hopes had soared that he was about to share his heart. The next day he'd been on the phone about an assignment, and the next day he was gone. She hadn't seen him again for six weeks. That was the way he was, and she'd learned to accept it. As long as he'd continued coming back to her, she'd been happy.

At some point, he'd decided she wasn't enough.

The stabbing pain sliced through her heart

again. What had she done? Why had he stopped loving her?

Drew stirred then and turned his head, emitting a gentle snore that made her smile. Light from the door illuminated his face. His cheeks were sunken and he was much thinner than normal. Beneath his naturally dark skin existed an unnatural pallor. Pinch lines of pain encircled his supple mouth. She longed to soothe them away with her fingertips.

He needed a shave, too, but then Drew had always gone for the scruffy whiskered look. She'd gone for it as well, head over heels.

Her eyes lingered for a moment on his face. Her beautiful, rugged, dangerous Drew. So deep and mysterious, so brilliant and creative and loving. He had many wonderful traits.

Her thoughts wandered back to the first time they'd met. After paying an enormous price for a group of his stunning photographs, she'd been thrilled for the opportunity to meet the man who could portray children with enough beauty and sensitivity to make her cry. She'd pictured an equally sensitive artist with a gentle and un-assuming demeanor.

What she'd met was a wild man with a cocky attitude, dark hair tied back with a leather strip, the tiny fish resting in the hollow of his darkly tanned throat. Dressed in tattered jeans, a denim jacket hanging casually from wide, muscular shoulders, the startling photographer had slowly removed his shades and devoured her with wolf eyes. It had been love at first sight.

Three whirlwind weeks later, over the furious protests of her parents, they'd married.

Her parents had been wrong. Drew was wrong. Now she was the only one left who believed in their marriage.

Deep in his sleep-drenched subconscious, Drew smelled Larissa's perfume. Sweet and expensive, just like the wearer. Pleasure washed through him, stronger than the throbbing, incessant pain in his body. Larissa.

Coming slowly out of his latest fifteen-minute nap, he hoped he hadn't been dreaming. He wanted to see her, to hold her. All of the agony of the last few days would disappear as soon as he held her.

Opening his eyes to slits, he saw with relief that she was, indeed, in the room. For a satisfying moment, he looked his fill, unnoticed. She stood at his bedside deep in thought, her attention focused on the wires and tubes dangling around him. She looked stricken, frightened, and he longed to take her in his arms and tell her everything was okay. A fierce protectiveness came over him, laughable because he was too weak to stand up, much less protect anyone.

His Larissa. Classy. Vulnerable. Gorgeous.

He wished for his camera.

Where was his camera anyway? He touched his chest, feeling for the pockets in his vest before realization crept in and he remembered where he was. He also remembered the other thing. He couldn't hold Larissa ever again.

The throbbing in his head reached a crescendo. She would have been so much better off if he'd made her a widow.

As if sensing his wakefulness, Larissa slowly turned, her gorgeous violet eyes liquid with unshed tears. Drew's guts clenched with the need to comfort her. He bit down on the sides of his tongue to hold back the words. Divorce was the right decision, regardless of his physical condition. Maybe because of it, too.

Mustering every bit of courage, he ground out the words, "What are you doing here?"

His hand lay limp across his chest. She reached for it, and her soft, silky fingers soothed more than any medicine. In a minute, he'd pull away, but right now, he just couldn't let go.

"I've come to take you home," she said.

He squeezed his eyes shut against the torment her words brought. *Home.* He didn't have a home.

Through clenched teeth, he said, "We're getting a divorce. I'm not coming home."

"I don't want a divorce, Drew, and you're in no condition at this point to pursue it."

He hardened his heart and his voice, saying as coldly as possible, "It's happening. Get used to it."

Her shimmering tears spilled over then and nearly killed him. Against his own will, he reclaimed her hand.

"Hey, don't do that. I'm not worth crying over."

Face sad, she leaned in and laid her head on his chest. He was sure his heart would explode.

"My ribs," he said, using the injury as an excuse, although her touch made him better instead of worse.

She jerked upright, all concern and contrition. "Oh, sweetheart, I'm sorry. I didn't think. Should I call the nurse?"

Her hands fluttered above him, afraid to touch but needing to comfort. A born nurturer, Larissa's sweet concern was getting to him fast.

Before he became a blubbering idiot, he said,

"I don't need a nurse. I need you to leave." He dragged in a painful breath. "Go home to Tulsa and forget me."

"I can't. I won't."

"Sure you will. Marry some great guy and be happy."

"I married a great guy, and I *was* happy."

He turned his face away. If he looked into those suffering eyes much longer, he'd be lost.

"I'm not leaving, Drew," she said gently. "And there really isn't anything you can do about that."

He squelched the grudging admiration for his smart wife. In his pitiful condition, he couldn't do much physically, but he knew how to make her miserable enough to leave. Oh yeah. He knew how to make other people miserable. That seemed to be his specialty. He squeezed down hard on the metal fish in his opposite hand.

Inside, he whispered, *God, if you care about her, make her go away.*

Not that he believed, but Larissa did. And if God was a good God, He'd know Drew was the worst possible choice of husbands for a wealthy socialite whose daddy was a squeaky-clean politician. She was a sweet, loving Christian who had too much to lose by staying hooked up with the likes of him.

But how could he make her go away without being cruel? Her inability to accept the inevitable was exactly why he'd planned to never see her again.

"We'll talk about this later," she said, her voice soft and shaky in the quiet. "Tell me about the accident."

"Accidents are not intentional."

"You know what I mean. What happened over there?"

He noticed how smoothly she'd sidestepped his demand that she leave him alone. All right then. He'd talk, tell her what she needed to know, and then try again to make her see reason. Right now, his head hurt too much to formulate a battle plan against a smart cookie like Larissa.

He related most of what he could remember, omitting that last horrible experience of flying away from the jeep. He hadn't asked but figured he knew what happened to the rest of the convoy. Not knowing was the better option at this point. He wasn't sure he could handle the truth right now.

"I guess I'm lucky to be alive." A little part

of him was scared about that, even though the practical portion thought the world would be better off without him. What if he'd died? Where would he be right now? A near-death experience made a man wonder about things like Heaven and Hell and eternity.

"It's more than luck, Drew."

"Still praying for me?" He knew she was. Every time they spoke on the telephone, even that last time, she ended the call with the same words, "I'm praying for you, Drew."

When she'd first gotten into the religion-thing, he'd thought church was a nice, wholesome hobby to keep her occupied while he was away. But Larissa took her newfound faith very seriously, and he'd noticed the change in her.

"Constantly," she whispered. And one look at her face told him it was true. She was probably praying this very moment. The idea both comforted and disturbed.

Did God even care about a sewer rat like him? If He did, why had life been so ugly? Why was he so filled with garbage that he tainted everything he touched, even his marriage?

But this was where the tainting ended. He'd hurt Larissa enough. He wouldn't damage her more.

"Thanks," he said.

She didn't answer, just sat there looking beautiful and uncertain. He felt like a jerk of the grandest order. The woman who was comfortable with senators and billionaires didn't know what to say or how to act, all because of him.

That he'd ever managed to win her love in the first place still amazed him. He, a nobody from nowhere, had won the heart of the sweetest, kindest, most beautiful girl in Tulsa society. He didn't fit with her kind at all, and they had let him know. Especially her parents.

"I guess your mother and dad were happy to hear about the divorce." The bitterness in his tone surprised even him.

She stared at him, lost for a minute. He was lost, too, his brain tumbling from one topic to the next. The only thing he could think of for very long was the pain in his body and the worse one in his heart.

"Mother and Dad don't run my life."

That was a laugh. She worked for her father, and couldn't say no to her spoiled, whining mother. In the more than three years that he'd known the Stone family, Drew had never done one thing that pleased them. Mostly, he didn't care.

But he did care about Larissa, and the estrangement brought her sorrow.

He'd do anything for Larissa. That's why he had to do this. "I'm tired. Maybe you should leave now."

She stared down at him, biting her bottom lip. "Go ahead and sleep. I'll just sit here beside you."

She wasn't making this easy.

"Go home."

"Not until I can take you with me."

The crashing in his temples grew louder.

"Get this straight, Larissa. I don't want to come home with you. Not now. Not ever."

"You have nowhere else to go."

That hurt. "Sure, I do."

"Where? What else can you do except come home to Tulsa?"

"Rehab. One of those in-patient places. I already talked to the docs." Not quite the truth, but close enough.

"Don't be ridiculous. We have a huge house. I can hire nurses or whatever you need. I can take better care of you than some impersonal rehab facility."

She reached out again, and he shrunk away. If she touched him, he'd lose his courage. With superhuman determination, he stared straight into her movie-star eyes and said, "Let me be clear about this. I can't stand to be in the same house with you anymore. Now, get out and leave me alone."

Abruptly, he closed his eyes and rolled his head to the side.

But not before he saw the stricken expression on his beloved's face.

Chapter Three

Larissa tossed a tiny Gucci bag onto a chair and collapsed on the bed at the nearest hotel. Fat raindrops, like tears, ran in rivulets down the window.

She was too exhausted for tears of her own. Emotionally and physically, she'd gone about as far as she could for now.

The meeting with Drew had been harder than she'd expected, and she hadn't expected an easy time. But she *had* expected him to want to come home to recuperate.

He was badly injured and disturbingly weak. The thought of him alone in an impersonal rehab facility tormented her.

How could he prefer such a place to their lovely, spacious home? The home they'd bought together? He loved that place as much as she did.

He just didn't love her anymore. At least that's what he claimed.

To hold back the cry of despair, she buried her face in a pillow.

Though she'd wanted to question why he had suddenly given up on them, after seeing his injuries, she was too concerned with his health. First, she'd get him well and then she'd fight him. She'd fight and she'd win because, even if it was arrogant, deep down she couldn't believe he'd stopped loving her.

Something was wrong, though. Terribly wrong.

The thought stopped her cold.

Insecurity reared its ugly head. Sometimes men strayed, even strong, steady, decent men like her father. Mother had never guessed, but Larissa had. A politician, like a photographer, traveled widely and alone. Good-looking, charming—both the men in her life would have no problem finding companionship outside the home.

No. She couldn't believe that about Drew. He might be secretive and mysterious in many ways, but he was faithful. She would know if he wasn't.

The other woman in Drew's life had always been his work. Could that be it? Was she cramping his freewheeling, traveling lifestyle?

No, that didn't make sense either. He came and went as he pleased already, even though she'd asked him to be home more often. His job had always come first, even before their marriage.

The familiar tune of her cell phone played and she fished the instrument from the bottom of her handbag.

A quick glance at the caller ID brought a groan. "Hello, Mother."

"Have you seen him?"

With a sigh, Larissa pinched the bridge of her nose. It was always like this—the tug of war between her parents, especially her mother, and her personal choices.

"I had a dreadful flight. Thank you for asking, Mother. And I'm exhausted. Yes, I've seen *him*. His name is Drew."

"I know that," her mother snapped. "Is he all right?"

"Do you care?"

"Larissa! That is no way to speak to your own mother. I have a terrible headache, too, but I wanted to check on my little girl before I took some medication and went to bed. Your happiness is the only thing that ever mattered to me." Her voice took on the whiney, childish quality Larissa had dealt with since childhood. "I wish you were here to make some of your delicious tea. I find it so soothing at times like this."

For Larissa's mother, Marsha Edington Stone, times like this occurred more or less every day.

Her discontented sigh huffed through the telephone lines, and Larissa imagined her sinking into the lush, reclining chair in the vast sitting room, one wrist dramatically tossed across her forehead like some eighteenth-century princess.

"What's upset you this time, Mother?" She'd long ago accepted the fact that Mother's troubles were far more important than her own.

"The luncheon was today. I don't know what possessed me to go without you. I'm not well enough, and now I'm paying for my dedication. All that chatter over who's going to chair next year's art council was too much. You're the logical choice, if they have any sense at all."

Mother had been sick and needy as long as Larissa could remember. Having grown up as the adored only child of a very wealthy oil man, Marsha was spoiled, although she did suffer from migraines and too much time on her hands. Larissa vacillated between pity and annoyance, but like her father, she never refused her mother anything. Larissa steered the conversation away from her mother's health. Marsha was a good person when she wasn't focused on herself.

"I'm sorry," Larissa said, automatically. Say it now, or pay for it later. "Please forgive my selfishness."

"I understand, honey. You've been under so much strain lately. It's no wonder you're edgy. As soon as this thing is over, you can get back to normal."

This *thing*, Larissa assumed, was her marriage. Her mother refused to believe Larissa could be happy married to Drew. She'd long planned a huge society wedding for her only child, and when Larissa and Drew eloped, the die was cast. There was no forgiveness in Marsha Stone for a perceived wrong, and since Larissa was her daughter, Drew remained the focus of the animosity.

Larissa's marriage, to her mother's way of thinking, was a dead horse. No use beating it.

"I do have some lovely news," Mother said. "Did your father tell you?"

Larissa's last conversation with her father had been terse to say the least. "I guess he forgot to mention it."

"We're going on a cruise to Italy. I am so

excited. I can hardly believe Thomas has finally agreed to get away from his office long enough to go. We've discussed it for years."

Larissa managed a laugh. "You make it sound as if you've never been out of the house."

Her parents had traveled to enough places to be U.N. ambassadors.

"Oh, you know what I mean."

Actually, she didn't.

"Why don't you come to Italy with us? Oh, darling, it will be such fun. A nice vacation is exactly what you need. We'll go to Venice and let some handsome Italian woo you in a gondola. Then we'll go shopping for the most wonderful wardrobe of Italian leathers. And by the time we return all this unpleasantness will be over."

"Mother." Larissa's anxiety level rose even higher. "I have to be here for Drew."

Silence hummed through the wires. Larissa could imagine the flat line of disapproval on her mother's collagen-injected lips.

"That's ridiculous." This time her mother's tone had a bite to it. "Stop being a doormat to this man. He's never been a husband. Traipsing all over the world and leaving you behind, embarrassed in society. Give him a divorce and move on with your life. Find a good man of our social standing and have a child. You're not getting any younger you know."

"Thanks for the reminder." Her biological clock *was* ticking loudly, and she hungered for children like a starving lioness. But she wanted Drew to be the father of those children, something he flatly refused to discuss. Children, he claimed, were not part of the package.

A headache threatened. She pressed a thumb and forefinger against her eyes. "I can't talk to you about this. I'm sorry." Lately, all she did was apologize.

"We used to talk about everything until you joined that religious group. I suppose they're behind this insane idea of yours to bring Drew home, instead of cutting your losses while you can."

Hoping to avoid a lecture, Larissa said, "I haven't had a chance to talk to anyone at church about this. It's all too fresh. You're my mother. I need you." Boy, was that ever true. "I love you."

"Well," Marsha sniffed. "I love you, too, honey. You're all that matters to me. I'm happy that you enjoy your church friends. Although in my opinion, you take this new religion fad far too seriously. Everybody gets divorced these days. Divorce isn't a sin, you know."

Larissa couldn't agree. According to her Bible, Christians didn't divorce even if they wanted to. And she most certainly did not want to.

But to the Stones, church was strictly a social institution, mostly used to better her father's political career. Though they attended occasionally as a family, especially during election years, they had never discussed personal faith in their home. She hadn't a clue what a relationship with Christ was about until her friend Jennifer had invited her to a Bible study last year after Drew had disappeared on one of his long treks to who-knew-where. Out of boredom and missing Drew so much she was willing to do anything, she'd gone. Within the month, she'd given her life to Christ and become a different person on the inside.

Her mother was still puzzled by her sudden devotion.

Though she'd tried discussing the topic with both her parents, the words had fallen on deaf ears. They said they were Christians "like everybody else" and that was that.

As much as she wanted to revisit the conversation, she didn't want to offend. Mother's sensibilities were so delicate.

"All I ask is that you think about it, Larissa,"

her mother was saying. "Daddy knows the best divorce lawyers in Oklahoma. Everything can be taken care of while we're in Italy. You won't even have time to be stressed."

"Drew is seriously injured. That's my concern right now."

"Daddy and I are not unfeeling beasts. If you are going to be stubborn about this, we will also arrange for the best rehab care available."

"Just as long as I don't bring Drew back to Tulsa. Right?"

There was a miniscule pause and then, "It's for the best, honey. Let Daddy take care of everything."

Mother made it sound so simple and bloodless. A vacation to Italy. She shook her head, depressed by her parents' lack of understanding. They were wonderful parents, who thought they knew what was best for their child.

Only she wasn't a child anymore.

Thoughts of Drew crowded in. Drew laughing and teasing. Drew charging into the ocean with her on his back. His expression intense when he spoke his love.

No matter what anyone said, she could not forget the beautiful parts of her marriage. They hovered inside her heart and mind like golden butterflies, too rare and special to release into the wild.

Somehow she managed to end the conversation, certain she hadn't heard the end of the Italy cruise. Then she fixed a cup of tea in the hotel coffeemaker. It wasn't her special blend of chamomile and raspberry, but the hot, sweetened drink warmed the chill in her bones.

Outside, a cold rain slashed the windows in incessant sheets. Inside, the hotel room was cozy. She climbed beneath the comforter, pillows propped behind her head, to drink tea and read the Bible.

In her haste, she'd left her own beautiful, Moroccan leather Bible at home. But the bedside table held the familiar Gideon version.

She flipped through the stiff book, finally settling on a page in Corinthians. Much of the Bible was still new to her and this was no different. She read out loud, hoping scripture would soothe her inner tumult. "Love is patient. Love is kind. It does not envy, it does not boast, it is not proud. It is not rude, it is not self-seeking, it is not easily angered, it keeps no record of wrongs. Love does not delight in evil, but rejoices in the truth. It always protects, always trusts, always hopes, always perseveres. Love never fails."

This was what real love was all about. God's kind of love.

As if the ancient words were written just for her, Larissa read them again and again.

"Love is patient," she murmured. "I can be patient with Drew."

And she could also trust and hope and persevere. Because God promised that if she would, love would never fail. She closed her eyes and smiled, ready to sleep now as she hadn't done in days. "Thank you, Lord."

Deep down, she understood what God was telling her. Just keep on loving Drew the way Corinthians stated. Keep loving. Because love would not fail.

The next morning, Drew awakened as soon as the weak winter sun slanted through the gap in the ugly green drapes. He was nervous. Larissa was going to fight him, and right now he was weak. Last night he'd tried to get up and head for the shower on his own. He'd made it to the end of the bed before collapsing like a Slinky. The nurses had scolded until, chastised, he'd promised to stay put.

He wouldn't necessarily keep that promise. He had to get out of here before he lost all courage.

A nurse arrived, and Drew went through the now familiar humiliation of being treated like a helpless infant. Ah, what was he saying? He *was* a helpless infant.

"Tell the doc I want to see him right away."

"Let's get you cleaned up first. I heard you had a pretty visitor yesterday."

He gave her a look intended to shut her up, but she was a cheeky sort. She pushed her glasses up on her nose and grinned. Drew ignored the insinuation. "Call the doctor."

"I heard you. The doctor will make his rounds soon. Right now he's in surgery."

"Great." He needed to get the rehab arrangements made today and get out of here. His frustratingly weak body was not cooperating. All he could do was wait.

As the nurse administered his morning ablutions, he stared at a painting on the far wall. What was it? A seascape? Mountains?

He squinted, trying to bring the blues and greens into focus. He blinked several times to clear the fog, and just that quick, the picture faded to gray and then to black.

His heart lurched. Cold fear snaked through him. He blinked again and again. Nothing happened.

He dropped his head back onto the pillow, fighting the panic. A groan escaped him.

"Mr. Michaels?" The cheeky nurse's voice held concern. "Did I hurt you? Are you in pain?"

Yes, though not the kind she meant.

For lack of a better excuse, he said, "My side," and grabbed for it.

No way was he telling the nurses about the unpredictable state of his eyesight. They might tell Larissa and then he was done for. If she thought for one minute that he was going blind, she would insist on taking care of him. He wouldn't saddle her with a cranky, worthless, blind photographer.

As professional hands skimmed over the bandage on his belly, Drew fretted. The doc had called the blindness transient. It would go away. It had to.

"There. Is that better?"

Though he had no idea what the nurse had done, he nodded anyway. "Thanks."

"You're welcome." She rattled around his bed and he waited for the sound to disappear before opening his eyes again.

A relieved sigh shuddered through him.

The world had somehow come back into focus.

He looked at his hands. They were shaking.

Outside in the hallway, people passed by

talking in low tones. So as not to think about the frightening blindness, he concentrated on the noises and waited for his doctor to arrive.

He didn't have long to wait. In moments, he heard the murmur of a male voice. But there was another voice, too. Larissa. He'd recognize that soft, educated drawl anywhere on earth.

Straining to hear, he caught bits and pieces of the conversation. "Mr. Michaels expressly asked me not to release his information to you, Mrs. Michaels."

Way to go, doc.

"But I'm his wife." Larissa's bewilderment was evident.

"He said you were going through a divorce."

"That's ridiculous. He must have gotten a concussion. We are not getting a divorce."

Drew couldn't hold back a smile of admiration. His woman was gutsy, that was for certain. She'd worked on her father's political campaigns long enough to know how to stand her ground.

The doctor's smooth, professional baritone answered, "He's asked me to make arrangements in a rehab facility here in D.C. I was just stopping by to discuss the particulars with him."

Drew clenched the sheet with both fists, reminding himself that the rehab was his idea.

Nevertheless, the thought of going to any institution filled him with dread. He'd been in way too many of them over the years, and probably should have been in others.

Flashes of his early teen years kaleidoscoped behind his eyelids. Boys' homes, therapeutic homes, group homes for troubled kids. He'd battled his way through dozens, fending off bigger, meaner boys, learning to steal and smoke. Learning which illegal drugs manifested what effect.

He'd tried everything and then some but had gone cold turkey after the fire….

He slammed the door right there. Sweat broke out on his body.

Not the fire. He didn't ever think about the fire.

He wasn't that wild, undisciplined kid anymore. He was Drew Michaels, professional photographer. Disciplined, controlled.

Jaw set, he bit down almost hard enough to break a molar. He could do this. He could go to a rehab center for a while and then get back to work where he belonged. And Larissa was not going to interfere.

Larissa stood outside Drew's room, glad to have encountered Dr. Spacey in the hallway so they could speak candidly. According to the nurses, he was the physician in charge of Drew's case.

"As sorry as we are to admit this, Mrs. Michaels," the bespectacled doctor said after listing Drew's many injuries, "our hospital is at capacity. We have to move patients out as quickly as possible—without jeopardizing care, of course. Your husband is well enough for release."

"He can't take care of himself." She stated the obvious.

"Not for some time, I'm afraid. His body has been through a lot, and he'll need several months of healing to get his strength back."

"That's why I'm here. I'm taking him home."

He cocked an eyebrow at her. "Have you spoken with him about this?"

"Do I have to?"

He looked amused. "Any man that didn't want to go home with you would be crazy, but he has a right to make that decision."

Larissa played the only card she had. She only hoped it worked. "I thought you said he had a severe concussion."

"That's true. He does. It's healing but he's still suffering some aftereffects."

Larissa filed that piece of information away.

Maybe the aftereffects were adding to Drew's reluctance. "Then, are you certain he's capable of making the appropriate decisions about his health?"

Dr. Spacey studied her behind black-framed glasses. Graying blond hair peeked out from beneath a green scrub cap. "What do you have in mind?"

"I can charter a plane whenever you say he's ready. We have a large home, easily accessible to the best physicians in the Southwest. I can hire nursing care, physical therapists, whatever you think he needs. No expense will be spared. I can give him much more personalized care than any facility in this country. If his head is giving him trouble, what better place than home and familiar surroundings to help him recover?"

Dr. Spacey rubbed a hand over the back of his neck, thinking. "You have a valid point. The best thing for your husband *would* be home and familiarity. Patients who've been through great trauma usually recover faster and with less psychological effect among family and friends."

Larissa felt a victory coming on. If she could just keep pushing, she might pull this off. "What do I need to do first?"

"Take him home and let him rest. The leg is non-weight bearing for at least six weeks anyway, but a physical therapist will have the details about that after you get him settled. He needs time more than anything else."

She smiled, weary to the bone, but satisfied that she was doing the right thing, whether Drew liked it or not. "I have all the time in the world."

The doctor patted her shoulder. "With that attitude, your husband will get along just fine. Let's go in and talk with him about this."

"But—" She stopped the protest rising in her throat. How did she tell him that her husband preferred a cold, sterile institution to any place with her?

She couldn't. She could only pray that she'd been persuasive enough here in the hall to counteract anything Drew might say in the next few minutes.

Dr. Spacey pushed open the door and went inside the room. There was nothing for her to do but follow, carrying the balloon and box of chocolates picked up at the gift shop.

What would she do if Drew refused to come home with her? How would she manage to convince the doctor that Drew was too ill to know what he was doing?

Whether he wanted to admit it or not, Drew *would* heal more quickly in her care. If she was injured, she would want someone familiar to care for her. She'd want to be home with her family, her friends, and her animals.

Drew had nobody else but her to turn to. Right now he needed her too much to refuse.

The man she'd promised to stand by in sickness and in health had nearly died. And she was not about to abandon him, no matter how much he protested.

Drew was seething. Seething. Larissa and his doctor were conspiring against him.

He stared at the squat surgeon standing over him. "Do you have that rehab set up?"

"Actually, your wife has a better plan."

He refused to look at Larissa, though he could feel her in the room. If he looked, he might weaken.

"I don't like her plan. Send me to rehab."

"You have a healing concussion. I can't be certain you're able to make the best decisions for yourself at this time."

"Meaning?"

"In my judgment, since Mrs. Michaels is your legal wife, she is the more appropriate decision-maker at this time. I'm going to dismiss you tomorrow morning into her care."

Drew shot upright but pain slammed him right back down. He lay back against the pillow, too breathless to speak.

"Everything will be fine, Mr. Michaels. Just be sure to see your doctors in Tulsa. Have them call for your records." He took a card from his shirt pocket and handed it to Larissa. If Drew had been able to get a good breath, he would have complained. This was his life. What was the matter with this crazy doctor?

Giving him a pat on the shoulder, the doctor departed. Drew was furious.

Larissa, her perfume pure torture, moved closer to set her gifts on the nightstand. A teddy bear balloon. Normally, he'd make some wise remark about that, but he was too angry. She was destroying his plan.

"I hope you're not upset." She fiddled with the balloon.

By now, he'd found his breath and his voice. "Just what do you think you're trying to pull?"

"Dr. Spacey and I were discussing your dismissal."

"Yeah, I overheard."

"Good. Then you already know. You are not

going to a rehab. You're going home. To our home where you belong."

"What did you do, convince him I'm crazy?"

She found where his fist was clenched against the bedsheet and tugged his hand into hers. He tried to resist, but for once, a woman was stronger than him. Imagine, too weak to resist a girl.

Violet eyes smiled down at him. "Get used to it, Drew. You married a woman who plans strategy for political campaigns. I outmaneuvered you."

"I'm not going back to Tulsa."

She bent down and kissed his cheek. He thought he'd die of pleasure. "Yes, you are. Tomorrow morning."

With an angry huff, he jerked his hand away. But he was no fool. He knew he'd been beaten.

He was about to spend the next few months convincing the woman he loved more than life, that he couldn't stand her.

This was not going to be fun. His stomach curled in anguish. Not fun at all.

Chapter Four

Drew jangled the tiny bell Larissa had placed at his bedside for that purpose. When no one appeared he threw the blanket aside and sat up. One hand under his cast, he gingerly swung the leg overboard—and then wished he hadn't.

Pain shot from his toes up his leg and into his brain in point-zero-two seconds.

With a hiss, he gritted his teeth to keep from screaming like a baby.

He sat there for a moment, one hand on his ribs, the other on his leg until his breath returned and the pain settled to a piercing howl.

His whole body trembled, a condition that infuriated him. If he could get his strength back, he could be mobile. Having never been dependent on anyone in his life, he hated the helpless feeling.

Five days back in Tulsa and he was still so mad he could spit. How had Larissa managed this? How had she manipulated him into living under the same roof with her again?

To make the situation even more difficult, she had moved him into the downstairs guest room and then surrounded him with luxury. She'd filled it with things he enjoyed, including a plasma TV mounted on the wall and a remote to open and close the drapes. A remote no less, so he could look out onto the backyard at will. She'd put enormous effort into making the room comfortable.

That was the problem. She was killing him with kindness and making him love her more, instead of less. He needed to get out of here and do it fast, but his body wouldn't cooperate.

No matter how much he growled and fussed and acted like a general creep, Larissa kept smiling and bringing him goodies. But he was a detail man. He could see the hurt she tried to hide, and he hated himself for putting it there. But he had to. Someday she'd thank him for it. Someday, when he could get out of her life for good.

Despising himself, he pressed the window remote and opened the drapes to stare broodingly at the yard.

Though Tulsa moved toward winter's end, the weather here was unpredictable. One day would be springlike, the next day snow or ice. Today was sunny, and the television claimed that temperatures were decent enough to be outside.

He'd spent too many years outdoors to appreciate much time inside a building. No matter how much he hurt, he was as restless as a windshield wiper.

Larissa's backyard, like her house, was pretty, even in winter. Birds pecked at feeders and flitted among the glossy green holly bushes. Wrought iron benches beckoned him to come out and play around the koi pond.

If only he had his camera equipment he could at least get some shots.

He rang the bell again, more insistent this time. Where was she? The more he annoyed her, the sooner she'd give up and send him to rehab. And he definitely was cranky enough to annoy anyone, even himself.

He'd slept away the first few days back, not caring much about anything. If his information was correct, he'd slept most of the last three weeks. But now he was awake and in a bad mood.

"Larissa!" he yelled and the effort set his ribs to aching.

As if she'd been standing outside the door waiting for him to hurt himself, his wife materialized. Dressed in trendy jeans and a sweater with too-long sleeves that was somehow exactly right on her, she took his breath away. Or she would have if he hadn't already lost it to the rib pain. Coco, the funny little Yorkie he'd bought two years ago to keep her company, trotted in behind.

"Do you need something?" She hovered in the doorway, anxious to help.

She'd been like this since his arrival and he was pretty tired of it. Sweet and kind and accommodating. Why couldn't she just hate him and get it over with?

"I'm bored." Coco trotted over and sniffed his toes. He wiggled away the tickle, frowning. "Go away, mutt."

Larissa's giggle washed over him as she came in and perched on a chair too close to his bedside. Her perfume came with her and tantalized him. All day long, he had to smell that delicious, irritating perfume.

"Okay. What would you like to talk about?" she asked.

His frown deepened. She was way too chipper. "Your attitude."

Her lush lips quirked at the corners. "*My* attitude?"

Okay, so he was the one in the foul mood. "Yeah, your attitude. Stop behaving like a servant. I don't like it."

Expression mild, she refused to let his crankiness rattle her. "How would you like me to behave? You aren't able to take care of yourself yet."

Like he needed that reminder. "Have the nurse stay longer. I don't want you in here all the time."

The last shot was hateful, so he braced against her inevitable flinch of pain.

It came, then quickly went as she shot back, "Dare I mention that you summoned me like some cranky king?"

Oh, yeah. He had. Lacking a reasonable answer, he did the only thing he could. He glowered.

Larissa got up to retrieve a pillow from against the wall. He'd thrown it earlier in a fit of frustration.

The woman amazed him with her serenity. How could she be calm when he was such a jerk?

"Leave it," he barked. "It's a *throw* pillow."

She picked it up, taking aim in his direction. Eyes narrowed, she said, "Don't tempt me."

His mouth twitched. Mixed with Larissa's grace and class was a good dose of spunk. Sooner or later, she'd get her fill of him.

"If I'm such a pain, send me to rehab. Get me out of here."

"We've had this argument." There was that annoying calm again. "You want to be here. You're just too stubborn to admit I was right. The home health nurses are doing a great job, as is the physical therapist."

So was Larissa.

"None of this changes the inevitable. I want out. You might as well cut me loose now and save us both the stress."

He hadn't planned to blurt that out, but the subject was on his mind most of the time anyway. The longer he stayed here, soaking up her kindness, the more restless he became. He was terrified of falling back into the habit of thinking of this place as his home. It wasn't. It was her house. Her town. Her everything. She deserved it. She belonged. He didn't.

Brocade pillow cradled like a protective shield between them, she refused to rise to the bait. "You need to get well. That's the only thing that matters right now. The rest can wait."

"So, you're saying, as soon as I'm well, you'll agree to divorce."

"That's not what I said." Distress twisted her face. He'd finally upset her. As a result, he felt lower than pond scum.

"Look, Larissa. I'm not trying to be the bad guy here. I'm just being honest." Sort of. He honestly wanted to convince the woman he loved that he didn't love her. How messed up was that? "I wasn't cut out for the married life. You knew it when you first laid eyes on me."

"But I fell in love with you anyway." She came to his bedside and laid a hand on his cheek. Her face softened and grew sad. "You once loved me, too. What happened?"

All it took was one touch from her, and he shuddered like a pathetic puppy. He tried to shrink into the mattress, anything to escape her sweetness. "Give me a break."

"Someone in Iraq did that already." She smiled and stepped back.

Resisting the smile, he deepened his scowl. "Not funny."

"The doctors say depression is natural after trauma this severe. We can call in a counselor if you'd like."

No thanks to that one. He'd had his head

shrunk plenty as a teenager, and the results had never been pretty. "I'm not depressed."

"That's why you're so cranky."

"I'm cranky because you won't discuss our situation rationally."

She blinked once, then glanced out the window, teeth sawing back and forth on her bottom lip. When she brought her attention back to him, she looked resigned.

"All right then. Let's discuss this. I can't even begin to understand what happened, Drew. The last time you were home, things were fine."

"No, they weren't. Things have never been fine. I'm gone all the time. I won't give you a family. Never." He emphasized that part. "I don't fit in your world. Your parents have fought us from the beginning. The pressure from them is killing you. You're miserable. Why can't you admit it and let go? We made a mistake. Let's fix it and move on."

"My parents make me unhappy. You never have."

Nothing like skirting the rest of the issues. "Until now."

She tilted her head in agreement. "Every marriage has ups and downs. If you'd only tell me what's wrong, we can get counseling. We can pray about it. We can talk it out. Work with me, Drew. We're worth it."

He hardened his heart against the sweet words. "You're a great lady, Larissa. You deserve a husband to love you and give you everything you want." *Kids*. "But that guy is not me."

"You could be."

He squeezed his eyes shut against the sorrow in her beautiful eyes. Through gritted teeth, he said, "I don't want to be. Now leave me alone."

Larissa didn't answer, and he could feel the hurt wafting off her like heat off sheet metal. After a few long, tense seconds, he heard soft footsteps leave the room.

Larissa fought anger for half an hour. Why was she putting herself through this? She should have sent him to a rehab the way he'd wanted. He was impossible. She must be out of her mind to think forcing him to stay here would make him love her again.

She took out a can of chunked chicken and thumped it onto the granite countertop. Tags jingling, Coco danced around her feet. The little Yorkie was great company, but the companionable dog wasn't Drew. Larissa wanted her husband with her all the time. She wanted a family. She wanted Drew.

"Help me know what to do, Lord. I'm so confused." Divorce was not scriptural but how long was a Christian supposed to keep trying when her husband didn't love her anymore?

Despair tugged like lead weight, but she fought away the feeling. The truth was, she'd keep trying as long as she could keep Drew in Tulsa. As awful as it sounded, she was almost thankful for his injuries. Otherwise, she might never have had this chance to make things right.

Larissa pressed her head against the cool cabinet door and tried to remember the verses she'd read in the hotel. All that came to mind was *Love never fails*.

At the moment love didn't seem to be working at all.

She hated this feeling. The tension between her and Drew could choke an elephant, and she didn't know what to do. Pastor Nelson at church offered counseling services, but until now she'd been unwilling to share her personal problems with anyone except her parents. And they only added to the stress. Maybe she should talk to someone who would listen objectively.

When Drew's sandwich was ready, she took the filled plate and a glass of milk to his room.

Drew had propped the pillows behind his head and was sitting up. The television played an action movie.

She'd expected him to be asleep again. He'd slept a lot since coming home, but he was wide awake. The circles beneath his eyes had lessened and the bruises on his face and arms, once black and yellow, were fading. All were reminders that Drew was not his normal self. Could the trauma be part of the problem? Could the horror of what he'd experienced cause him to behave so wretchedly? The man she'd married had never been like this. He'd been warm and funny, a little cynical and arrogant, but he'd treated her like a queen.

"Hungry?" she asked quietly.

His head rotated in her direction. He looked tired and drawn, as if every conversation stole more of his strength. Guilt pricked Larissa's conscience. He didn't need arguments right now. She'd vowed not to discuss anything troubling until he was better, and she'd already broken that promise. Drew needed to heal, physically, mentally, even spiritually.

Sometimes the line between fighting for his health and fighting for their marriage blurred.

She would have to remember that his health came first.

"Not very." He motioned toward the night-stand. "Put it there. I'll eat it later."

Drew normally ate like a horse, but not since the injury.

He extended a hand, then changed his mind, letting it fall to the sheet instead. "Thanks for the sandwich."

As if regretting the earlier outburst, his tone was quiet. Larissa wished she could understand what was going on in that complicated mind of his.

"Will you be all right for a little while?" The nurse had already come and gone for the day. "Mother called."

"Sure." A flicker of amusement flashed in bad-boy eyes. "Give her my love."

"Drew," she admonished, but in truth, the spark of personality pleased her. This was the old Drew.

His face lit with mischief. "Sorry."

He clearly wasn't. The hostility between Drew and her parents had begun the first time they'd met and continued to this day. Drew didn't fit her parents' country-club image of a proper husband for a state senator's daughter. He was far too unpredictable and rough around the edges, and he wasn't impressed by their money and prestige. The very things that appealed most to Larissa were the ones her parents despised.

"I promised to take Mother to the beauty salon."

Drew didn't bother to ask the obvious question because they'd covered this ground before. Her mother seldom went anywhere alone. It made her nervous and brought on migraines.

"Go ahead. I'll be okay." He glanced toward the window with a longing gaze. "I might even run away."

They both knew he could no more run than he could fly.

Larissa smiled. "If you do, be back in time for dinner. I have some fun planned."

His eyebrows lifted in question, but she didn't share her sudden inspiration.

"I've asked Cody from next door to sit with you," she said instead.

"I don't need a sitter."

Too bad. He was getting one.

"Cody's a great kid. You remember him, don't you?" Cody and his sister Kelli, along with several other neighbor kids frequently used her indoor pool. When Drew was away, Larissa enjoyed the company.

"Sure."

"I'm not going to leave you alone."

"I won't really run away." He made an X on his chest. "Cross my heart. Does Cody play video games?"

"All twelve-year-old boys play video games. To hear him tell it, Cody is the king."

"Then, he's my man. Send him over. I hope he has NFL football."

"If you'll promise to be good and stay in bed, I might even bring you a present."

"A present, huh? Let me think." He rubbed his bottom lip. "Considering how bad my ribs hurt today, you got a deal."

Larissa walked out of the room feeling much better than when she'd entered. Now, if she only knew what had caused Drew's sudden mood swing.

Three hours later, ears still ringing from her mother's usual diatribe, Larissa returned to the white villa-style home in south Tulsa. She loved this place. Following an afternoon of listening to her mother's advice, she couldn't wait to get back here to her own little world. She and Drew had chosen this house together shortly after their elopement, and it had become her safe haven.

They had both fallen in love with the house on sight, but for different reasons. She loved the Italian architecture, the koi pond and pool house. He'd been enamored of the spacious open floor plan and the way natural light filled each room with a warm glow. Together they'd added a hot tub, chosen furniture, repainted the living room, and had set up a darkroom in the basement, thrilled with their compatibility in so many important things.

She was sad now to realize that, during their whirlwind courtship, they'd never once talked of children or considered the effect of his travel on their marriage.

Still, those had been wonderful days and this villa was filled with happy memories. If she had her way, there would be many more, including children. But first, she had to change Drew's mind about a lot of things. Starting with the ugly topic of divorce.

Just thinking the word brought on a weight of despair so heavy she could barely keep walking. Her stomach hadn't stopped hurting in days.

Dropping her keys on the hutch, she shucked her coat and wished the ever-present worry would fall away as easily. Putting on an intentionally happy, though false face, she went to check on Drew and Cody.

Cody sat on the floor, video controllers in hand, fighting aliens from outer space. Drew was sound asleep, the lines of fatigue a constant reminder of how weak and ill he was.

The boy looked up and shrugged. "Zonked out."

They kept their conversation low, and Drew didn't stir.

"You must have beaten him."

Cody grinned. "I did."

Ruffling Cody's blond hair, Larissa returned the grin and dropped several bills into the boy's lap. "Drew's not a very good loser."

And neither was she, a trait she'd learned from her father's many election campaigns. No matter how grim the forecast, a Stone never backed down and never quit.

Cody shut down the video machine and stuffed the money into his jeans' pocket. "Drew's pretty fun. Kind of shaky though. He got real tired after a couple of games."

Larissa's heart squeezed. A man who could trek the Congo for days on end had been felled by two video games.

"I appreciate your help, Cody."

"No problem. I'll babysit him anytime you want." He shrugged into his coat. "Well, except when I'm at school. Mom makes me go there no matter what."

Grinning back into the exasperated blue eyes, Larissa saw Cody to the door, watched him run across the wide expanse of her lawn into his yard. Then she headed back to the kitchen to put away the groceries.

Thanks to one of her parent's housekeepers and a gourmet cooking class, Larissa had learned to enjoy cooking. Since bringing Drew home, she'd put that love to good use. His body needed all the help she could give it.

Coco trotted in, looking for a treat. Larissa tossed her a doggie cookie.

From the sick room came the tinkle of Drew's bell. Buoyed by the hope that he'd awakened in the same good mood, she stashed the last box of pasta in the cabinet and headed his way.

When he saw her instead of Cody, he said, "I thought my babysitter had abandoned ship."

"I sent him home. You were out cold."

He scrubbed a hand over his face. "I don't know what's wrong with me."

"Rethink that statement."

"I mean, I know what's wrong. I just don't know why I'm taking so long to recover."

"Well, let me see." She ticked the problems off on her fingers. "You had a concussion, lost several pints of blood, broke your leg in more places than you have bones, lost your spleen, had shrapnel removed from various locations, including your head. Really, Iron Man, I don't know why you don't get out of that bed and run the triathlon."

His grin was adorably sheepish, and she wanted to kiss his scruffy face. She wouldn't, of course. He didn't want her affection and until he did, she would go right on loving him at arm's length.

She was trying hard to believe that love never failed, though, in all honesty, she couldn't understand why her prayers hadn't already been answered. God didn't approve of divorce. So, why didn't he instantly change the situation? She'd asked him to about a thousand times.

"Where's that present you promised?" Drew asked.

She stuck one hand on a hip and teased, "What if I forgot it?"

His eyes narrowed to slits. "You didn't. I know you."

Yes, he did, sometimes better than she knew herself. "And I know you, too, big baby. Here's your present." She handed him the shopping bag. "I hope it's the right one."

He tore into the bag like a kid on Christmas, his face intense with excitement as if a gift were a rare treat. Drew always reacted with the same endearing pleasure that made Larissa want to buy him everything.

"Oh, man." Stunned and pleased, he lifted out the camera. Almost lovingly, he turned it over. "A Nikon. My favorite."

His dark gaze flickered up to hers and held. What she saw in those depths made her heart flutter. Was it only gratitude? Or something more?

"I know," she said, thrilled to please him. He'd loved that camera. Of all the equipment he owned, he preferred this particular one. "And since you lost the other one…" Not wanting to remind him of that terrible day, she let the statement slide.

Already lost in the new camera, Drew checked every detail. "It's perfect, sweetheart," he said, giving her a quick, sweet smile. "Thank you."

Whether intentional or not, the endearment was almost as good as a kiss. Pure happiness zipped through Larissa, a rarity of late.

"I thought you might occupy yourself by snapping some photos around here. Maybe you won't be so grumpy."

His expert fingers quickly readied the camera for use and took aim at her.

Head tilted in mock-annoyance, she was secretly thrilled. Why would he want photos of someone he planned to leave? The little ray of hope glowed brighter.

She opened the drapes so he could try out the zoom.

Then, eyeing the uneaten sandwich on the table, she said, "You play for a while. Then I have another surprise."

Drew grinned. "Two in one day? I may perish from the excitement."

The gleam of white teeth against dark skin was stunning. He should take his own picture. Larissa knew she'd love him even if he were ugly, but he was so wildly beautiful, just looking at him was a pleasure.

Drew didn't know what to do. His wounded body had put him in this spot and his aching heart was dying a slow death. What was wrong with Larissa? Why didn't she hate him yet? It seemed the more he misbehaved, the nicer she became. Surely, she would wake up some morning soon and realize what a loser she had married. If he could convince her of that, he could walk away knowing she would be all right.

Coco hopped upon the bed. Drew aimed the Nikon and snapped. Larissa would get a kick out of a framed photo of Coco, red bows in her ear tufts, toenails freshly painted.

Dismayed at his need to please his wife even now, he tilted his head back and stared at the crown molding. As quickly as that, the world dimmed. The blue wall faded to black. Stunned and scared, he yanked his chin to level and blinked rapidly. The blindness hadn't happened since the hospital. He'd thought he was cured.

Pulse pounding against his temples, he blinked over and over. Slowly the room returned to normal. His pounding heart took a lot longer.

Setting the Nikon aside, he rested back against the pillows to stare around the room. He was afraid to close his eyes again.

An hour later, he was still lying there, listening to his heart beat and soaking up every visual detail when Larissa came sashaying in, a picnic basket on her arm and a big smile on her face. She'd applied fresh lip gloss—a touch of pink.

Just enough so Drew couldn't take his eyes off her. She had a beautiful mouth, full and perfectly bowed, and incredibly kissable.

He remembered the last time he'd kissed her. Six months ago.

By sheer force of will he managed to glance away. But there was no real escape.

Larissa climbed onto the side of his rented hospital bed, bringing with her the scent of freshly spritzed perfume and fried chicken. He couldn't decide which smelled better. He was shockingly hungry.

"What are you doing?" he asked. "What is this?"

She set the basket between them. Thank goodness. "A picnic."

He tried to scoot up in the bed away from her, but his ribs screamed in protest. Short of breath, he gave up. "I don't think that's such a good idea."

"Too bad. I want a picnic. We can't go outside, you can't get up, so we're having it right here. A bed picnic." She shot him a cheeky grin. "Don't argue. You're trapped, and I am in charge."

Try as he might, he couldn't keep from grinning, too, although his was grudging. "Who knew you were such a bully?"

As if she did this every day, Larissa opened

the basket, flapped a red-and-white checked tablecloth onto the bed, and started setting out an array of colorful plastic wear.

"I'm a campaign strategist. I make a living bullying people—in a nice way, of course." She handed him a chicken leg. "Work on that while I get set up."

His taste buds rejoiced as he bit down on the crispy meat. "I can see why your dad never loses."

She laughed, and the sound was like music. He loved making her laugh. A woman like Larissa should always have a reason to laugh. Thanks to him, she hadn't had much opportunity.

"Potato salad?" she asked.

"The works. I'm starved."

"That's a first."

"So's this picnic."

"Fun, huh? A picnic without ants."

Drew quirked an eyebrow at the tiny dog. "Unless she qualifies."

Larissa laughed again, and Drew was pretty much done for. All men were saps when a woman laughed at their stupid jokes. Larissa was great about that. Ah, what was he thinking? Larissa was great about most things. And right now, he didn't have it in him to hurt her feelings.

Not today anyway. Let her have her picnic and her fun. He'd get back to business tomorrow.

For the next half hour, he gave in and let her pamper him. He even let himself enjoy it. The only strained moment had come when she wanted to pray a blessing on the food, but he'd survived that.

She chatted away as if he'd never demanded a divorce or behaved like a jerk, filling him in on details of the people they knew, the changes in Tulsa, the play she'd watched at Christmas without him. Though plays were not part of his bizarre upbringing, he'd come to share Larissa's appreciation of the arts.

At one point during the picnic, he made the mistake of touching her. Without thinking, he'd leaned forward to wipe a cookie crumb from the corner of her mouth. Their gazes locked and held. After a long, aching moment, she turned her cheek into his hand and kissed his palm.

And then she'd backed off, cheeks aflame as if they'd never kissed before.

He didn't know which would kill him first, her sweetness or his guilt.

What had he been thinking when he'd married her, a wealthy, socially accepted politician's daughter who was as good as he was wicked?

Well, there was his answer. He hadn't been thinking at all. He'd been in love, frantically trying to freeze the moment in time, wishing it could last and knowing full well nothing good ever did.

He'd been right, too.

Ah, but he'd loved her so much. Still did, a fact that scared him to pieces and made him vulnerable. He hated vulnerable. Usually, he hit the road when the feelings came. This time he was stuck.

Poor Larissa. She'd been completely innocent to the kind of man he was. And as they always did, the same old lousy things had happened. He'd wanted to be her hero, her everything. Instead, he'd become her absentee husband, a loser who was too afraid of the past to make a decent future with the finest woman on the planet. He'd taken something as good and pure and special as love and found a way to damage it.

Bad blood always told. Change his name. Hide his crime. Deny his past. It didn't matter. Bad blood always told.

If Larissa's God really cared for her, why had He allowed Drew Michaels to ever get near her?

He sat back against the headboard and

watched her gather up the remains of their honey-sweet picnic. He was tired, both inside and out, but Larissa's company made him forget the constant pain.

She glanced up a time or two, made a few silly remarks that brought a smile. "There's a good movie on Pay-Per-View tonight. You up for it?"

She wasn't going to let him off easy, was she?

"I think I can fit it into my busy schedule."

As tormenting as it was, he would soak up all the love he could. For the hard times that would come later, long after she had seen the light and cut him loose.

Chapter Five

A wheelchair wasn't a particularly convenient mode of transportation, but Drew had learned to maneuver it like a chariot racer as soon as he had stopped feeling like soft-set Jell-O. The most exciting part of his day was rolling quietly up behind Larissa when her back was turned and waiting for that little startled squeak of awareness.

Pathetic but true. His adventurous life was reduced to photographing black-capped chickadees and begging the kid next door for a game of video NASCAR.

Larissa, on the other hand, was a regular whirling dervish. Constantly in motion, she somehow managed to take care of a crippled, cranky husband, pamper her whining mother, attend church and field dozens of work-related phone calls each day. He'd urged her to go back to work in her father's office, but so far she hadn't.

As long as she was out and about, he was fine. It was when she came home that he was in trouble. Then his steel magnolia of a wife would waft into the room, a fragrant flower to his emotional cesspool, and his inner battle started all over again.

Leg elevated, camera in his lap, he wheeled the chair through the spacious house, careful not to ram his foot into anything. Coco jingled alongside, spoiling his chance for a surprise attack.

Winter was loosening its hold early as it often did here in Tulsa. The first green daffodil shoots were poking up in Larissa's flower garden. Soon, he'd set up a time-lapse camera and see what he could discover.

He found Larissa in the sunny living room arranging fresh flowers on a side table. They had two living rooms, a waste, he thought, because this was the one most used. The family room, she called it, dubbing the other as formal. Here, double French doors opened to a native rock patio and divided walkway leading out to the pool house and down to the koi pond, the hot tub and the gardens. In nice weather, she threw open the doors to meld the outside with the inside.

"I'll be glad when I can get in the pool." He looked longingly through the glass. "Such a shame to have an indoor pool and a hot tub and not be able to use either."

Larissa poked a pink carnation into the vase and reached for a yellow one. "Another few weeks and you'll have the cast off. Be patient."

"Getting blown up forces a man to be patient," he groused.

"And you've fought it every step of the way."

"I'm not good at convalescence. Being stuck in one spot makes me antsy."

She tapped his arm with the flower. The petals felt as soft as the kiss she'd placed in his palm during the bed picnic. He'd laid awake long into the night thinking about that. He should never have allowed the picnic.

"That's an understatement," she said mildly.

He didn't know why, but after a while in the same place, he grew uneasy, as if the world was catching up. After a childhood of constant change, common sense said he'd want roots. Weird that life hadn't worked that way. He wanted to stay put. He just couldn't.

"The living room smells nice."

"Tonight is my turn to host Bible study."

"Oh." Bible study. Like he knew anything about that.

She poked a yellow flower into the vase. After a beat, she glanced at him and said, "You could join us."

There was no missing the hope in her voice, but Drew shook his head. "Not a good idea."

He'd met some of her church pals and they were all right, but he felt out of place in their midst, as if they shared a secret he wasn't privy to. Besides, hanging out with Larissa and her friends wasn't exactly the way to break up a marriage.

Or maybe it was…. Maybe she needed to see how poorly he fit in decent company.

Larissa was an active woman. She had clubs and committees and charities. She biked and golfed and took classes. That's why the whole church-thing baffled him so much. She didn't need the time-filler.

"Finding Christ changed my life, Drew," Larissa said softly. Though she set the flowers in the center of the table, turning them this way and that, Drew knew her real focus was him. Her religion had become that important. "If you'll let Him, He'll do the same for you."

Nothing could change him. Hadn't every social service and therapeutic foster home in Oklahoma tried? He couldn't even change himself.

"I don't know much about God except that a lot of wars are waged in His name."

A fact which had always irked him. People killing people in the name of some deity. Didn't make sense.

"Don't blame God for that. Why do you wear a Christian symbol if you don't believe in God?"

"This?" He touched the ichthus. It felt warm in the hollow of his throat. "I never said I didn't believe."

"You never said you did, either."

She stopped fidgeting with the flowers and came closer to his chair. He had the most foolish urge to pull her down onto his lap and kiss her until she cried uncle. He wanted to make her laugh and get that starry-eyed look that made him feel so strong and powerful and manly. He wanted to nuzzle her neck and hear her say she loved him more than Hershey Kisses. It was their pet phrase, started on their honeymoon. He'd bought six bags of the chocolates and covered her with them while she slept. He'd wanted, he'd told her, to shower her with kisses for the rest of their lives.

What an idiot he'd been to think anything that precious could last.

"I haven't been a Christian very long, Drew, but I wish I could share the experience with you." She tapped her heart. "Something happened to me in here. I don't even know how to explain it, but letting Jesus into my life filled an empty spot."

He knew about empty spots. A hole in his soul, one counselor had called it. Psychic wounds. He'd heard plenty of psychological mumbo jumbo about why he behaved the way he did, but none of their talk had ever filled the gaping emptiness. He couldn't imagine how reading a Bible and singing a few hymns would make any difference.

The only thing that ever helped was going into a dangerous assignment, as if the violence there externalized the powerful emotions raging inside him. Only then could he forget who he really was and where he'd come from. He could forget how much he missed his brothers. Most of all, he could forget the faces of those who had died because of him.

"I'm glad for you, Larissa. If that's what makes you happy."

She touched his arm. A touch, but he soaked

her in like the parched deserts of Africa. "He can make you happy, too. He can heal our marriage. If you'll let Him."

"What time are your friends coming over?" he asked, annoyed that his throat was rusty.

"Seven."

He glanced at the huge sunburst clock over the fireplace. "I'd better make myself scarce then." He started to wheel away. "Any snacks I can steal to take with me?"

"Magic cookies bars. But only if you stay for Bible study."

"You cheat."

She only smiled.

In the end, he'd chickened out and rolled back into his den like some bear in hibernation, lap filled with goodies he'd snitched from the kitchen. She'd prepared enough snacks to feed the whole church and then some.

Her look of disappointment niggled at him.

Ever since her conversion, as she called it, she'd talked too much about religion. Well, not religion really. God. Jesus. The Bible.

He pointed the remote toward the TV and channel-surfed. A hundred and forty channels and nothing worth watching. He pressed Off.

Restless, he ate a few grapes and made a game of catching them in his mouth. A few plunked against the carpet and Coco scurried after them, sniffed and turned up her nose.

"Come here, girl." He patted his lap. The Yorkie obeyed. "Guess it's me and you tonight. Want a cookie?"

Larissa wouldn't approve, but he broke off a bite anyway.

"Don't tell your mom," he said, and grinned when Coco yipped as if she understood.

The little dog was a golden fur ball of pure silk. Red painted toenails matched the bows sprouting from her pointed ears. Larissa thought it was cute. Drew thought it was funny. Coco received better care than some kids.

He knew that for a fact.

He'd never had a dog before unless he counted the strays Collin had tried to keep. Poor mutts never stuck around. There wasn't enough to eat. As an adult, he'd been gone too much to care for an animal.

Sometimes he wondered if he'd bought the dog as much for himself as he had for Larissa.

When the cookies were gone, Coco hopped down and trotted to the door.

"Traitor," Drew said to her departing back. "I

know your tricks." She'd sneak into Larissa's party and beg for more treats.

He'd thought about sneaking in there himself. Rather, he'd considered behaving like a jerk, so Larissa would see how unfit he was to be with her friends. In the end, he'd backed out. Even a loser like him couldn't stand to embarrass Larissa that way.

Without the dog for entertainment, he thumbed through a couple of photography magazines and a sports book. Boring. He tossed those aside and flipped through the DVD collection. Most he'd already seen.

He was pretty sick of video games, though he wouldn't tell Cody that. Drew didn't have much experience with kids, but Cody was pretty cool to hang out with on a dismal Saturday while Larissa was off pandering to her mother.

In a few more days, his ribs should be in good enough shape to use the crutches. Then he could drive. He couldn't wait for that day to come. The only place he'd been since arrival was to the doctor's office.

He rolled the chair to the window, looked out. A marbled-white moon dangled overhead but the stars were invisible. Out across the wide expanse of lawn, security lights illuminated an enormous mimosa tree. The breeze wobbled the bare limbs back and forth. He could almost smell the piercing sweet blooms, though they wouldn't come until June.

By then, he'd be gone. He had to be.

Restless, but sick at the thought of leaving, never to return to the only place he'd ever known joy, he wheeled away from the window. He'd known it would be like this if he returned. Agony to be here. Agony to leave. They would both have been so much better off if Larissa had never come after him. But his wife was a politician's daughter. She had trouble accepting that the votes were in and the race was lost.

He spun the chair around. Gray spots speckled the air. The world blurred, fading in and out.

He sucked in a breath.

The spots hovered and wavered. He watched them as he would a horror movie, with disbelief and a sense of unreality. This couldn't be happening. Not again.

Afraid to touch his eyes, afraid to move, he sat frozen in fear. He could hear the blood pound in his ears.

"God, please don't let this happen."

Whether the words were a prayer, he couldn't say. But he didn't know what else to do.

He was losing his wife. Now he was losing his eyesight, too, and with it, the career that defined him as a human being.

After a few awful minutes, the hazy, tormenting curtain lifted, and he breathed again.

Sweat beaded his upper lip. He turned on every light in the room.

What would he do if the lights went out for good?

Maybe he should tell his doctor, but what was the point? The docs in D.C. had said there was nothing they could do.

He longed to tell Larissa, to share the worry. But he couldn't. If she thought he was going blind, she'd fight the divorce even harder. That's just the way she was. She'd hang on to a useless, worthless photographer out of pity. And he wasn't about to saddle her with a physical *and* an emotional cripple. More than ever, if he was going blind, he had to set her free.

If he was well enough, he'd be out of here tomorrow before she discovered the truth. Not just about his eyes, either. All of it.

Right now, though, he had to get out of this room. Being alone in the dark had terrified him as a kid. And he and his brothers had been alone in the dark more times than he could count. A few times he'd been locked in a closet for throwing a fit. He hated the dark.

What would it be like to be in darkness forever? A shudder racked him from head to toe.

He shoved the wheels of the chair into motion and rolled to the closet for a pair of aluminum crutches. Previously, the pressure on his ribs and abdominal incision had been too much. But no way was he going in there among Larissa's friends in a wheelchair. This would be a first. If he could do it.

Using the crutches as leverage, he stood on his good foot. Getting up wasn't difficult, but the ribs worried him.

Slowly, he eased down onto the padded rests. A pulling pain rippled beneath his arm and circled his chest. He drew a short breath.

Yep, still hurt.

Teeth gritted, he made his way across the bedroom, stopping at the door to lean and catch his breath. He was weaker than he wanted to be.

After a moment he continued on, hip-hopping on the quiet hall carpeting.

The doorway to the family room seemed a million miles away. Who knew this house was so big?

Arriving in the alcove outside the meeting, he

stopped once again to catch his breath. He was panting like a dog, his ribs threatened to come out of his chest, but there was no way he would go back to that empty room.

Voices drifted out of the family room. He eavesdropped for a few minutes until able to enter without making a spectacle. Memories of the child he'd once been, standing on the outside looking in, pushed him forward.

Pasting on a smile that probably resembled a grimace, he thump-thumped into the room. An empty chair waited like an oasis at the end of the couch—if he could get there.

Larissa had prepared a place for him in case he changed his mind. His throat tightened with the sweetness of such a gesture. He never expected anyone to consider him, but Larissa always did.

A momentary hush fell over the conversation. Ten pairs of eyes turned in his direction. Larissa popped up like a jack-in-the-box, long crinkled skirt swirling around her ankles as she rushed to his aid.

"Drew! Honey, what are you doing?" Her expression was a mix of pleasure and concern. "Why didn't you call me? Are you okay?"

He wished she wouldn't have asked him that.

"Great," he muttered through clenched jaws. Even his eyeballs were sweating with the effort.

She stepped closer, lowering her voice, to save his overactive pride. "Do you need help?"

He glared at her. "Not yet. But you'd better get out of my way before I embarrass us both."

Which was exactly what he should do, be rude and crude and obnoxious. But Drew didn't have the strength.

Hovering at his elbow, Larissa followed along as he thumped to the chair. Sweat bathed his face and slicked his palms.

With gratitude and a grunt of triumph, he slithered into the chair.

Larissa watched him for a moment, anxious, and then whirled toward the group. "Most of you know my husband, Drew."

The happiness in her tone almost finished him off. Was it that important that he hang out with a bunch of religious people he barely knew?

Annoyed to feel out of place and uncomfortable, he nodded to the assembly.

A murmur of polite greetings circled around him. Several men offered a handshake. He'd met one of them, Mark Bassett a few times at the country club. Someone asked how he was feeling. He managed a raspy answer, lying through his teeth. He wasn't fine. He was about to die. Every bone in his rib cage hurt. His lungs screamed for air. His body wobbled like a broken hula hoop, and he was sweating like a pig.

But he'd made it. If he was anything at all, Drew Michaels was a survivor. He'd made it in here and he'd make it out. Proof that, when the time came he was still man enough to do what had to be done.

No matter how much it hurt.

As the group settled back into their study, he checked them out. Though he didn't remember all the names, he remembered details. The blonde with the asymmetrical face, the guy with the pencil mustache who looked like an actor in an old movie, a married couple who could pass for brother and sister. He offered a smile to Larissa's best friend, Jennifer, a red-haired spitfire who had once actually approved of him. Now she glared back as if he was pond scum.

Well, wasn't he?

He was hurting her best friend. He deserved her animosity. No way would she understand that his insistence on a divorce was not intended to hurt Larissa, but to set her free from a lousy future.

He sneaked a peak at Larissa, hovering in the archway between the family and dining rooms. She wore the strangest expression: Surprise, admiration, pleasure, worry. He didn't want her to worry.

Breath returning to normal, he gave her a wink. She smiled.

Suddenly, he forgot about the terrifying blurriness. Forgot about the agonizing journey from the bedroom. He even forgot about the pain in his ribs and all the reasons he shouldn't encourage her.

"We're doing a word study tonight, Drew," Mark said, leaning forward. The dude was a little too preppy for Drew's taste, but he seemed sincere about his faith. Drew pretended interest.

"Jesus is called the Prince of Peace," Mark went on, "so we wanted to find out what that means to us today, as believers. We're learning about peace."

Drew figured he could use a healthy dose of that.

Though he felt awkward and out of place, no one seemed to notice.

Larissa scooted a kitchen chair right next to his and opened her Bible for him to share. He probably should maneuver away, but moving from this chair now was impossible. Trapped by his own making, he settled in to listen, acutely conscious of his wife's nearness.

From what he could tell, Mark was the leader because he talked the most. "According to the book of John, Jesus' peace is not the kind of peace the world talks about."

"Then what is it?" Jennifer asked.

"I found a place in Philippians," Larissa offered, sounding unusually shy. "I really like it."

Drew had seen her reading the Bible at night. It kind of freaked him out.

"Read it."

She flipped the thin leaves of the Bible, generating a puff of air that stirred her perfume. "Here it is. Philippians 4:7. 'And the peace of God which surpasses all understanding will guard your hearts and minds through Christ Jesus.'" She laid her manicured fingers over the page. "To me, that means no matter what happens or how difficult the situation, you can have peace on the inside, in your heart and mind, knowing that everything is going to work out for the good."

Was she talking about their marriage? Was that why she kept on trying even after he'd made it clear he would not change his mind about a divorce? Was her religion causing all this resistance?

"A peace that passes all understanding," Mark was saying. "Pretty cool."

Peace in any circumstance. Didn't make sense to him. But apparently his wife believed it. His curiosity got the better of him.

The session went on and Drew listened more intently than he'd intended, but he didn't open his ignorant mouth. No way. Though a street kid with little formal education, he'd read widely and traveled enough to pick up a lot of information. He was a quick study at just about anything, but this religion business was uncharted water.

A couple of times he touched the necklace and wondered about the bit of scripture engraved on the back. Someday he might ask someone. But not Larissa and not tonight.

After a while, when Drew's head buzzed with overload, the group broke for refreshments.

The woman with the asymmetrical face, one that would make an interesting photo, came over for a chat. Now he remembered. Her name was Amy.

"We were all sorry to hear about your accident. Our church has been praying for you."

Drew nodded, uncomfortable. "Thanks."

"Could I bring you something to drink?"

After an hour of stress, he was as dry as the Sahara. A bunch of Christians were more nerve-racking than photographing lightning.

"I'm good. Don't trouble yourself."

"No trouble at all. I'm happy to do it." Amy darted off toward the kitchen where Jennifer dug in the refrigerator, handing out Cokes. Drew was aware that Larissa's best friend avoided him like the bird flu.

Larissa, meanwhile, was at the bar, deep in conversation with Mark. Sandy brown hair, blue eyes, laugh crinkles, and a great tan, the guy was all right. Nice. Probably even had blue blood. Much more Larissa's type than a rambling photographer from the back alley.

Drew narrowed his eyes, seeing his wife and the Bible teacher in a new light. Larissa should have married a man like Mark. In fact, Mark might be the right man to step in once Drew was out of the picture. He was a lawyer, part of Larissa's social set, a good Christian, and well able to give Larissa everything she wanted and deserved. If memory served, the guy had lost a wife to an accident some years ago. He was probably ready to settle down and have a few rug rats running around the house.

Drew slid lower in his chair, adjusted the

heavily braced leg, and studied the conversing pair.

Yep. Mark was a great candidate to step in once Drew was gone.

"Here you are." Amy returned, bearing a can of pop and a plate of cookies. He didn't have the energy to admit he'd eaten half a dozen already.

"Thanks."

Amy settled onto Larissa's chair and peppered him with questions. Before long, he was sharing his travels, his photo shoots, interjecting the truth with enough funny comments to make the woman laugh. He laughed once, too, but pain hit his rib cage, so he decided not to do that again.

In spite of his resolve not to, he looked around for Larissa. He couldn't seem to help himself. This time she was chatting up the married couple as they took their leave.

After shutting the door, she turned his way, but before he could catch her attention, Mark said something to her. She laughed. The musical sound sprinkled the air like confetti.

Annoyance zipped through Drew. Larissa was his wife and he should be the man making her laugh. Not some preppy tennis jock with a great tan and a law degree.

He shook his head at the irony. One minute, he wanted to marry her off to the guy and the next he wanted to punch Mark's lights out for making her laugh.

Sheesh.

He took a long, stinging drink of Coke.

He was hopeless.

Chapter Six

As soon as the last guest left, Larissa flipped off the porch light, set the deadbolt lock, then leaned against the door. Her shoulders ached with tension.

The Bible study had gone great, but Drew's unexpected appearance had rattled her nerves. He was barely strong enough to get in and out of the wheelchair. What if he'd fallen and reinjured something?

Most of her friends had no idea that Drew wanted a divorce, but she'd been afraid he might say something. Or worse, that he and Jennifer would get into a confrontation. Jen was a great friend and a good Christian, but her temper sometimes overrode her common sense. Right now, she was furious with Drew.

Larissa glanced toward her husband, still in the straight-backed chair where he'd collapsed two hours earlier. He was staring at her, one knuckled hand to his scruffy cheek.

Even though he looked exhausted, his wolf-eyed gaze gave her butterflies. It always had.

Dear Lord, I love him. Please make him see reason.

She started cleaning up the room, taking the empty pop can and plate from the end table next to him. "What possessed you to get on those crutches tonight?"

He quirked a lopsided smile. "Got to start sometime."

"I nearly had a heart attack when you came wobbling through that archway."

"That makes two of us."

"You're really proud of yourself, aren't you?"

"Yes, ma'am. I'm mobile. Tomorrow, the car."

She harrumphed. "Think again, mister."

He offered an empty glass. When she reached for it, he held on, holding her there while he said, "How do you feel about Mark?"

Where had that come from? "He's a friend."

"That's not what I meant."

He watched her with such intensity that she swallowed, understanding too well what he asked. He was trying to shove his own wife at another man!

She yanked the glass. "I resent that implication."

Drew shrugged, a casual dismissal of her feelings that cut deep. "Mark's more your type."

"You're my husband, Drew, till death do us part."

"In other words, you'd be better off if I'd died in that blast."

She clumped the gathered dishes onto the bar. "Don't do this."

A spray of cookie crumbs fell to the tile. Coco rushed in to clean up the spill. Who cared about Italian tile or cookie crumbs? Her husband wanted a divorce and nothing else mattered. "Why can't you see that we have something beautiful and good, a relationship worth fighting for?"

Drew was silent. She turned and was troubled at the stark yearning in his expression.

"Drew?" she whispered, reaching toward him.

He blinked and the expression was gone, so fast she almost blamed her imagination. Almost.

She moved toward him, tempted to fall against his chest and cry out all her pain and love, to make him admit that he still cared for her. His injured ribs, and the fear of rejection, held her at bay.

She touched his arm, but he shifted away. She squinted at the rock-hard line of his jaw. All this time she'd believed he avoided her touch out of loathing. Now she wondered if the cause was another emotion entirely.

Dropping her hand with a sigh, she said, "It's late. You need to rest."

"Rest won't change the inevitable, Larissa." His voice was cold. "I'm filing for divorce as soon as I can get out of here."

The words still ripped like a chain saw. She held up a hand.

"Let's not have this argument tonight." She couldn't bear it. The Bible study had been so encouraging and now this.

She found a couple of dirty napkins and tossed them toward the garbage can. Between praying and worrying, she wouldn't sleep again tonight.

"We've never had this conversation at all. Every time I bring it up, you change the subject or run away. Get it through your head, Larissa. I'm out of here. It's over. I'm gone. The only thing keeping me here now is a broken leg."

Her whole body jerked at the vicious assault. Biting back a cry of despair, she asked the inevitable question. "Is there someone else? Is that why you want a divorce?"

She hated the way her voice trembled, but she had to know.

Eyes hot, she watched Drew's face. He wouldn't lie about something this important. She was certain of that.

He stared at her a long time, a muscle over his cheekbone twitching. Finally, he rasped out, "No. Never."

Weak with relief but as confused as ever, she asked, "Then why?"

"I've told you." He gazed toward the fireplace, avoiding her eyes. "I don't want to be married anymore. It cramps my style."

Cramped his style? When had she *ever* done that!

Suddenly, the pressure of the last few weeks came to a head. Like a volcano, she erupted, all the anxiety and fear and hurt boiling over.

"Well, I've got a flash for you, hotshot. Commitment is about sticking with something even when it's not fun anymore." She stabbed a finger at him. "And believe me, you are no fun at all right now. I know you don't want to be here with me. You've made that very clear. But you're still my husband, and I'm not turning my back on you or our marriage."

"But you'd like to, wouldn't you?"

His tone was too quiet and too hopeless. Blasting him wouldn't accomplish a thing.

Exasperated, she went back to cleaning the room. "I can't talk to you."

The room hummed with tension while blood roared in her ears. Drew remained on the chair, but Larissa refused to look at him again. Let him stew. Let him sit there and think up ugly things to say. He could sit there forever for all she cared.

A wadded napkin thunked against her arm.

"Hey."

She whirled on him. "Don't say another word right now."

"I've never seen you so fired up."

"I've never had a husband try to dump me before." At the admission, emotion clogged her throat. With the iron will that helped her deal with a fractious mother and her father's difficult electorate, she swallowed it down. She was not about to cry in front of him again. Never again.

Drew pulled a hand down his face. "Peace?"

She bent and yanked the napkin off the floor. "A little late for that."

"I didn't mean to ruin your Bible study." His

tone had changed from cold and hard to calm and solicitous, and she had no idea why.

"You didn't." *But you're trying to ruin my life. Our lives.* And she refused to discuss it anymore tonight.

She returned the chairs to the kitchen, then straightened the couch pillows. All the while, Drew remained silent, brooding.

Larissa checked the door locks and turned off all the lights except for the family room and hallway. With one last glance at her puzzling, exasperating husband, she started toward the stairs.

"Hey."

One hand on the smooth, golden banister, she stopped but didn't turn around.

Drew didn't speak for another long moment. When he did, she understood his hesitancy. "I think I need some help."

He'd made the trek to the living room, but he couldn't make it back.

Larissa turned around. "You seem to crave independence from me. Why not start now?"

"Smart aleck," he said mildly, his expression soft and troubling. "Come on. Be a sport and help the poor crippled guy."

"In other words, you need me, so you'll put up with my company."

"Something like that."

"You are impossible."

"That's what I've been trying to tell you. I'm a user, Larissa. I'm no good for you."

He was the most bewildering human being on the planet. But she loved him anyway. She'd brought him here to recuperate and for a chance to save their marriage. As much as his cruel words hurt, she wasn't ready to throw in the towel.

With a resigned shake of her head, Larissa went to retrieve the wheelchair.

The trip down the hall to the Bible study must have taken every bit of strength and determination he could muster. When Drew set his mind to do something, he seldom failed, a truth that both comforted and terrified. He would get well, and without divine intervention he would also leave her for good. He was that stubborn.

She wished she could understand why God was letting this happen to her. Wasn't she trying as hard as she could to be a good Christian? Her marriage hadn't deteriorated until after she'd accepted Christ.

"Sit still while I straighten your bed," she said. When the sheets were tightened and the pillows fluffed, she patted the mattress, but kept her distance. There was a limit to the rejection she could tolerate in one night. "I'll bring you some ibuprofen."

"Make that a double," he grunted.

On arms bulging with muscle, he pushed up from the chair to stand on one leg. Halfway up, he started wobbling like a bobble-head. His dark skin paled. His upper lip erupted in perspiration.

Larissa's heart twisted with pity—and with sadness for a man who hated to ask for help, especially from his own wife.

Hurrying, she stuck a shoulder under his good arm. "You have *so* overdone."

He was twice her size, but she managed to heave and shove until he tumbled onto the bed. Unintentionally, she fell with him, her arms trapped behind him.

Their faces were inches apart. Larissa's pulse beat a rat-a-tat-tat against her collarbone. Drew's dark, secret eyes searched hers, his manly scent as familiar and wonderful as ever.

As if the sound was torn from deep in his soul, he groaned, "'Rissa."

In that one word, she heard a longing he refused to admit. Though she couldn't under-stand the source, a battle raged inside him. She waited, hoping for more.

Finally, voice gruff, he said, "Let go."

"I can't. I'm trapped." Not that she was sorry. Nor was she trying to rectify the problem.

"Yes," he answered, sadly. "That's exactly what you are. Trapped."

Then, as if he couldn't stop the action, he stroked her hair back, looped a stray lock over one ear. At the exquisitely tender touch, Larissa melted.

"What are we doing, Drew?" she whispered. "What's happened to us?"

A lump, hot and heavy as a brick, formed behind her breastbone. She leaned closer to kiss him, to reclaim what was hers. He rolled to the side, releasing her, but not before she recognized what he was trying to hide.

She worked in campaigns. She understood better than most what body language and the eyes could say that words didn't.

Drew still cared for her.

Long after the house quieted and Coco abandoned him for Larissa's upstairs room, Drew lay awake staring into the darkness. Tonight had changed him. And he was scared out of his mind. He wished his body would heal faster. He wished to be five thousand miles away.

Most of all, he wished to be upstairs with his wife.

His determination had almost crumbled as she'd leaned over him, warm perfume wrapped around his senses like a cozy blanket.

He was a loathsome excuse for a human being.

Over and over, her wounded expression played in his head. He'd said some hateful things tonight. How much more could she take before throwing him out on the street?

Tossing the cover aside, he slid out of the bed and grappled for the crutches. Painfully, he maneuvered to the stairs and alternately crawled and hobbled to the top. Larissa's room, *their* room, was directly in front of him. Ribs screaming in protest, body distressingly weak, he wobbled to the closed door and rested against it, gathering both his strength and his courage. He didn't even know why he'd come up here.

And then he heard her.

Soft muffled weeping, as if her face were in a pillow. Heartbroken cries of despair. He could hear her voice, too, but couldn't make out the words.

Was she praying?

He squeezed his eyes shut.

Oh, God. And he meant it. Having to hurt her killed him. *Killed him.*

She was the best thing in his life. The only human being, other than his brothers, who had loved him in spite of his failings.

Emotion bubbled up inside, threatening to overflow and drive him to his knees. He longed to offer comfort, to promise her the world and everything in it. Anything to make her happy again.

Perhaps he should go in there, beg her forgiveness, and reveal the whole truth—that he was afraid to let her love him, afraid that he would never be what she needed. Afraid she wouldn't want him once she knew the truth.

He lifted a hand to knock, then let the clenched fist fall to his side.

Leaving her was the most unselfish thing he'd ever do in his life.

He'd come this far. He couldn't back down now.

Tomorrow he'd begin rehab in earnest. In a few weeks, his body would let him leave. If only he could be sure his heart would do the same.

Larissa noticed a change in Drew following the night of the Bible study. Within the week he was hobbling around the house on crutches and by the next his ribs tolerated an outing or two. He still tired easily, but she was relieved to see him healing.

The physical improvements weren't the only changes she noticed, though the others were less subtle. She wasn't foolish enough to think one Bible study had influenced him that much but one never knew. Whatever had happened, he'd mellowed. To her vast relief, he said no more about divorce, though it hovered between them like a bad case of halitosis. She wouldn't complain about the respite even though his silence felt like the calm before the storm.

And now, after that one sweet, aching moment, she believed he still loved her. His words said no, but his eyes said yes. And that alone was enough to keep her going. Though she'd cried herself to sleep that night wondering why he kept a wall between them, something was stirring inside Drew.

She felt him watching her and sometimes when she turned around he would look away, pretending to be otherwise occupied.

If he would only share what troubled him, maybe they could resolve their issues. But Drew didn't trust her enough for that.

Now that he'd wounded her so deeply, she

was afraid of what else he might do. And yet, she couldn't give up hope.

Her mother had called her a fool yesterday. The words cut like a razor, deep and drawing blood.

"Stop catering to a man who doesn't want you. The whole town is talking."

In other words, Mother's friends.

"They wouldn't know my business if you didn't tell them," Larissa had replied, and then she'd left her parents' home, too upset to stay and help with hanging the new drapes. Her mother wouldn't forgive that inconsiderate action for a long time. She'd already phoned twice today, insisting on her daughter's help.

Larissa glanced out on the patio to see Drew maneuvering one crutch at a time down the rock steps to the koi pond. Early spring had arrived, filling her backyard with sweet-scented lilacs and a wild abundance of perennials in need of taming. Camera swaying around his neck, Drew had mentioned feeding the koi while she worked on the flowers. Coco trotted happily along beside him, pausing now and then to gaze up in adoring concern. Her master's slow movement puzzled the little dog.

Now that Drew was mobile, as he called it, he spent considerable time with the fish.

Restorative, he said, to sit in the gardens and wait for birds and butterflies to land in sight of his camera lens or to snap action shots of the koi at feeding time. He'd even named the three orange males Groucho, Harpo, and Zippo, after the famous old comedians.

For a man accustomed to erupting volcanoes, civil war, and other wild adventures, watching the fish swim couldn't be too fascinating.

Still, he relieved her of their care as much as possible, for which she was grateful. Cleaning the pool was the downside of enjoying the colorful fish.

Slipping into a hooded jacket, her bucket of gardening tools in hand, Larissa went to join him.

Crutches propped against a chair dragged close to the edge, he tossed food into the water, one piece at a time.

"The irises are taking over," he said, nodding to the tall purple heads around the edge of the pool.

"Spring does that." It occurred to her that Drew hadn't been home long enough to experience their backyard in spring or any other season for that matter. "They start spreading. If I don't divide a few, they'll crowd out the fish."

He bent to the water and pulled one up.

Holding the lavender flower next to her face, he shocked her by saying, "This one's the color of your eyes. You have beautiful eyes."

Larissa held her breath as Drew tucked the iris behind her ear and let his hand linger on the fall of hair streaming over her shoulder.

A smile bloomed inside. This was the Drew she knew and loved.

Six months ago, when he was home, he had said those same kinds of romantic things. He'd told her she was beautiful and precious. Then, she'd been confident of his love, though he'd seldom spoken the words. And she had loved him with such fierceness that she'd mourned for days each time he left. What had happened between then and now?

The waterfall tumbling over the flat rock sides of the pool was music. The scent of spring was fresh and moist and promising. She ached for a similar renewal in her fractured marriage but didn't know what else to do.

Except pray. She could always pray, and remember that love never fails. Even though it had so far.

"Some of the neighborhood kids are coming over later to swim," she said, not wanting to move lest Drew's tender mood wither and die with the culled flowers. "Will you keep an eye on them?"

"Rug rats," he said, though his response was harsher than his treatment of the kids. He liked them in a gruff sort of way. "Where will you be?"

"I have some things to do for Mother."

He dropped his hand, disappointing her, his opinion of her errand clear. "What impending disaster is it this time? The patina on her silver spoon needs polishing?"

"Drew," she admonished softly. Sometimes the requests *were* petty excuses for attention. "We didn't finish hanging the new drapes." She didn't mention why. "And she's asked me to interview maid applicants."

"Didn't you do that a few weeks ago?"

"Consuelo didn't iron the way Mother likes."

"Criminal offense. No wonder she's getting the ax." He tossed a grain of feed into the pool. "Don't your mother's demands ever get on your nerves?"

He didn't know the half of it.

"Sometimes," she admitted.

"You don't show it. Even when she calls with some nonsensical crisis that will resolve on its own, you jump and run."

"Wouldn't you have done the same for your mother?"

His expression turned to stone. He lapsed into silence and stared down at Groucho making kissie faces on the surface of the water.

Contrite to bring up an obviously painful topic, but curious, too, at the reaction, Larissa touched his arm. The dark skin was taut beneath her fingertips.

"Why don't you like to talk about your family?"

"They're dead," he said harshly.

"So is my Grandma Sadie, but Dad and I still tell funny stories about her all the time."

"Yeah, well…" He let the topic hang. Forearms on his knees, he flicked a single bit of fish food to Harpo and watched the bubbles send ripples across the surface.

"Surely, you have some good memories." Larissa held her breath. She was pressing again and fully expected Drew to grab his crutches and limp off toward the house. If he was well, he'd head for the telephone and by tomorrow he'd be at the airport. It happened every time she ventured too close.

But why not press? She was losing him anyway.

To her surprise, he didn't back away.

"I had two brothers," he said softly. "Awesome brothers." The words carried the bitter-sweet ache of love and loss. "All for one and one for all. That was us."

Larissa smiled, thinking of the cute little boy Drew must have been. She would love to have a baby just like him. "Sounds as if you read the Three Musketeers."

"I don't remember." His mouth curved in a sad smile. "Collin came up with the idea. He was the smart one."

Collin. Drew had never mentioned any of his family by name before.

She kept quiet, hoping he would go on in that rambling, reminiscent manner. She wanted to know about the fire that took their lives and how he came to be the only one not present at the time. She might even ask.

A breeze ruffled his longish hair and he thrust the dark, loosened locks straight back from his forehead.

"Losing my brothers was the worst thing that ever happened to me."

On her knees beside the pool, Larissa pulled another iris and didn't look at him. Even though her insides tensed with the need to know, she spoke casually as if the answer was really no big deal. "What were they like?"

Asking Drew for personal information was as precarious and unpredictable as playing in the crater of a volcano.

Silence reigned for a few seconds and Larissa figured the conversation was over. She pulled another stray flower, adding it to the bucket for discard.

A pebble of fish food plunked the water in front of her.

"We built a fort. Our secret hiding place in the woods behind the school. Collin brought stray dogs there." He laughed softly, sadly. "They ran off."

Pleased and emboldened, she sat back on her heels to look at him. "And your other brother?"

His eyes flicked to hers, but instead of secret darkness she saw light. "Everybody liked Ian. He was too little to keep up when Collin and I took off for the fort. Collin carried our stuff. You know, kid junk. I carried Ian. He was so skinny, I could put him on my back and run the whole way."

"Most boys would find that pretty annoying, wouldn't they? A tagalong brother too small to carry his own weight."

He twitched one shoulder. "I didn't mind. It was Ian."

"He ain't heavy; he's my brother?" she asked, quoting the old song.

"Yeah, something like that, I guess."

She saw the depth of love he'd had for his siblings and understood a little better why it pained him to discuss them. The loss of those he'd loved so much had left a huge void in his life.

"Once we had this old bike," he went on. "Ian climbed on the handlebars and I peddled like crazy, showing off."

She tapped his bare toes.

"Imagine that. You showing off." His cocky attitude was one of the things that had first attracted her.

He shot her a sideways grin. "I took a bump too fast and Ian went flying. Hit a rock the size of Toledo. Busted his head open." He touched a spot above his temple. "Scared me to death. I thought I'd killed him. Dumb kid wasn't even mad. Instead, he was upset because I was. He kept saying it was okay, it was okay." He shook his head. "Dumb kid."

"Those are good memories, Drew. Memories to cherish."

His gaze found hers and held steady. Something flickered in his expression, a relenting of sorts. After a bit, he said, "In all the bad, I guess I'd let the good get lost."

"I love hearing about your brothers. About you. I like thinking of you as a little boy."

She was no psychologist but any intelligent being with half a heart could see that Drew hid things, maybe even from himself. Arrogant, stubborn, secretive. Did those attributes hide a deeply wounded child?

"You know everything about me that matters," he said.

"No, I don't. You've always held back a part of yourself."

"Why do women have to dig so deep?"

She cocked her head and kept her answer light. "Is that a sexist remark?"

He tossed a grain of fish food at her. "I've never talked to anyone before about Collin and Ian."

The admission sent a ripple of pleasure straight to her heart. She'd longed for this kind of husband-and-wife communication.

"You can tell me anything, Drew. *Anything.*"

For a second, he looked bewildered, and then his face hardened as if keeping a distance took great effort.

Grappling for his crutches, he pushed up from the chair. Larissa remained on her knees beside the pool, bucket filled with wayward irises. As Drew maneuvered around her, she stopped him with a hand on his foot.

"Drew." She gazed up into eyes as dark and mysterious as midnight.

"What?"

"Don't run away anymore, Drew. I need you."

He squeezed those mysterious eyes shut, and when he opened them again, he groaned, "Ah, 'Rissa."

Her heart thumped once, hard, before the loud chatter of children's voices shattered the moment.

The neighbor kids, Cody and Kelli, came around the side of the house, followed by three other children in the same age range.

With a beleaguered sigh, Drew turned to greet the newcomers. Larissa's hope filtered to the ground like falling leaves.

"Hey, dudes and dudettes," Drew said to the kids. "What's happening?"

The little girl giggled. She batted long eyelashes. "You said we could swim. Is now okay?"

At eight, Kelli was a fair-haired beauty with eyes as blue as robin eggs. Drew was a sucker for the little girl although he would deny it to the death.

"Sure," Larissa answered. "I have some things

to do inside, but Drew will be out here. He won't mind playing chaperone. Will you, Drew?"

She turned in time to catch the roll of his eyes heavenward. "Looking forward to it."

Larissa suppressed a giggle. "I'll bring out some snacks and the cell phone, just in case."

"Yippee," he said wryly, but his eyes sparkled with humor.

Getting faster all the time on his crutches, he followed the gaggle of children. He'd traveled maybe ten yards when he suddenly stopped and wavered.

"Drew?" Pulse in her throat, Larissa dropped the gardening bucket and rushed forward. "What's wrong? Are you okay?"

Leaning heavily on one crutch, he rubbed a hand across his face. "Just a little wobbly. I'm good."

But as he started forward again, Larissa couldn't shake a new awareness.

For one split second before she'd reached him, Drew had looked afraid.

Chapter Seven

Drew prowled his bedroom, restless and worried. Larissa would be back soon. She'd gone into her father's office for a few hours of strategic planning—whatever that entailed. With his cast off and the ribs decently healed, he was well enough the nurses no longer came, and the physical therapist only stopped by every other day.

If he wanted to accomplish anything, now was the time.

A few days ago he'd made a tactical error. He'd talked about Collin and Ian. It scared him that he'd told Larissa so much, as if the few sentences could resurrect his sordid past and ruin his present.

He was getting far too comfortable with

Larissa, letting his guard down that way. The trouble had started the night of Larissa's Bible study and hadn't let up.

But he'd been thinking about something she'd said that night. Thinking and wondering.

Larissa was a Christian. Her faith didn't allow for divorce. Now, he wondered if religion was the only reason she wanted to hold on to their crippled marriage.

He'd never planned to marry. Never thought he was capable of loving someone other than himself, considering his lousy childhood. Larissa had changed all that. And now, because of her religion, she believed she was stuck with him forever. He loved her too much to allow that. But unless he made the break soon, he wasn't sure what might happen.

Maybe the concussion had done more than blur his vision.

He'd almost given that away, too. A couple of times he'd been tempted to tell her about the fearful episodes of blindness. But his pride wouldn't let him. He knew her. Out of pity, she'd fight the divorce twice as hard if he went blind.

A shudder wracked his body. A blind photographer.

Time to do something more proactive than beat

Cody at video racing. The doc had said the episodes should disappear with time. They hadn't.

He limped to the bedside table and fished around, coming out with a fat phone book. In the yellow pages, he found a long list of ophthalmologists, though he wasn't even sure an eye specialist was the right kind of doctor. He had to start somewhere, but he didn't want Larissa to know. Somehow, he'd find a way to the doctor's office when she was out and about. A cab, he supposed, though the crutches put a crimp in his mobility and wore him out in a hurry. His stamina stunk.

As he lifted the telephone receiver, he flexed his ankle, grateful that the pain was now only soreness. He'd be off the crutches soon.

He heard the front door open and Larissa's voice call, "Drew?"

He slammed the receiver down.

The call would have to wait.

Later that afternoon, Larissa went in to straighten Drew's room. She noticed the open phone book, and out of curiosity glanced at the page. Not surprised to find he was looking up doctors, she *was* surprised at the names circled in pen. All were ophthalmologists.

Eye specialists?

Gnawing on her bottom lip, she wondered. What else was her secretive husband hiding?

Sunday morning dawned cool and cloudy. Drew awakened with grim determination.

He'd never cared for Larissa's mother, and today he liked her even less. She was to blame for his latest dilemma.

Yesterday, dear Marsha had stopped by. Again. Lately, the woman was underfoot all the time, but yesterday she'd hurt Larissa's feelings, and Drew was still red hot about that. The woman had berated Larissa for spending too much time with her church friends. Like an idiot, Drew had hobbled into the living room and announced that he was going to church with his wife. Her mother had been so horrified, she'd shut up and left.

Now he had to follow through.

With a determined grimace, he hopped into the bathroom. The things he did to himself.

He showered, shaved and dressed, though he didn't own a suit and wasn't in any shape to go shopping. Larissa's church friends might look down their noses at his attire, but let them. He wasn't interested in impressing anyone anyway.

With more effort than he'd expected, he forced a pair of dark gray chinos over his cast and found a blue shirt Larissa had given him for Christmas. His weight loss made the silky-smooth Italian button-down a little loose, and he needed a haircut, but the mirror said he looked pretty good anyway. He hadn't been this dressed up since their impromptu wedding.

For a few pleasant seconds, he remembered that day. He'd actually been cocky enough to think he could pull off the grand charade and marry a princess without anyone ever knowing he was the frog.

With a self-deprecating laugh, he shook his head.

Delusions of grandeur. But ah, what a great three years they'd enjoyed.

Whether she admitted it or not, Larissa had to know their marriage was an error in judgment. He'd known all along, but hadn't accepted the truth until she'd brought up babies. Then he'd heard the death knell.

Well, whatever. Today, he was going to do one last nice thing for her. And maybe for himself. The whole church/religion thing weighed heavily on his mind lately. He'd even taken to praying about his eyes. Not that it did any good, but he kept thinking God would feel sorry for Larissa and heal him for her sake.

After spritzing on a light dose of cologne, Drew went to find his wife, oddly anxious to see her reaction. He'd looked like day-old roadkill long enough.

The phrase gave him pause. Roadkill.

He'd been lucky. Some of the others in the convoy that day hadn't been. Larissa claimed God was protecting him for some reason known only to Him. Drew didn't know about all that, but he was grateful to be alive. He rubbed an index finger over the little fish around his neck, thinking. Lately, he'd been thinking about a lot of serious things. He supposed a near-death experience had that effect on everyone.

The scent of coffee drew him toward the breakfast nook. Larissa loved the espresso machine and all those exotic types of coffee beans.

He found her standing with her back to him, stirring sweetener into a cup. Her long, dark hair hung in a gleaming sheet from a fancy clasp at the crown. He was suddenly overtaken by the powerful urge to touch the silky hair and to smell its clean, flowery fragrance. He wanted to wrap himself in her presence, in her scent, her warmth and to forget death and destruction, blindness and pain, all the other ugliness that resided outside her arms.

The urge was so powerful he wobbled. To rein in the startling need, he cleared his throat. "Good morning."

She spun around, spoon in hand. Her violet eyes lit up.

"Wow," she said, delighting him.

"You like?" He preened a little. Well, as much as a man with a bum leg could preen.

For one glorious minute, he basked in Larissa's warm honey gaze. Then, quicker than the wink of a shutter, he realized the futility and looked away.

"Are you really going to church with me?"

She hadn't believed him. He should have expected that.

"I said I would." The answer came out gruff and cranky. Thumping up to the bar, he levered onto a stool.

She lifted one finely arched eyebrow. With an inner wrench, Drew remembered the silky feel of that brow beneath his fingertip. With the discipline that made him a patient photographer, he reined in the memory.

"I thought you only said that to upset Mother," she murmured.

He grinned. "Maybe so. But I said it, so I have to do it."

Those glowing, soft eyes sparkled. "Yes, you do. But I wish you'd go for more reasons than to annoy Mother."

"Maybe I am. You said God protected me. I figure I owe Him."

"I might even take you out to lunch afterwards."

Uh-oh. "Better not."

Her face fell. He couldn't stand that.

Backpedaling, he said, "What I mean is, I'll take you. Well, technically, you'd be taking me, but…" He offered his cutest grin and shrugged.

Her disappointment lifted instantly. She handed him a cup of coffee. "I know just the place."

"Yeah? Where?" He was trying to be jolly about the whole church thing, but the hint that she might turn this into something more worried him. "Maybe I should just stay home. You can go out with your friends."

She aimed her coffee cup at him. "Oh, no you don't. You are not backing out on me now." She grinned. "I'll tell Mother."

He gave a mock groan. "Sneaky."

"Yeah, well, you should have expected that.

Besides, you're all dressed up. Can't waste a good-looking man."

Liking her compliment more than was wise, Drew pointed a finger. "If you're a praying woman, better pray now. I'm driving."

He limped out of the room with the musical sound of her giggle in his ears.

Drew had photographed temples, cathedrals, mosques and shrines all over the world. He'd been in and around any number of churches, but he wasn't prepared for Sunday morning worship service at Larissa's church.

A few people stared. Others introduced themselves. Most paid him no mind at all. Larissa's klatch of friends, however, gathered around and seemed genuinely glad to see him. Though he found their welcome strange and unsettling, he was also warmed by the friendliness. Even Mark shook his hand and invited him to join an outing next week.

Having considered the church group to be Larissa's friends and not his, Drew had expected to feel left out, like a fifth wheel, but he didn't. His wife's popularity drew him into the circle.

As they entered the sanctuary, choosing a place near the back out of consideration for his disability, Drew couldn't take his eyes off his wife. No wonder she had a bevy of friends. She was beautiful inside and out.

He wondered if he'd ever told her that.

Today, she wore heels with a simple print dress shot with the violet color of her eyes. A single amethyst dangled from a silver choker in the hollow of her throat. Wide silver bracelets adorned one wrist, showing off her long, slim fingers and manicured nails.

He had wanted to please her this morning but, as strange as it sounded, he was the happy one.

The service began and though he was uncomfortable both emotionally and physically, he liked the music. Then the preacher got up, a short dynamo of a guy, and told everyone to open their Bibles to the book of Matthew. He'd never owned a Bible in his life, so Larissa scooted closer to share. He anchored one side of the book on his knee. She anchored the other on hers so that they touched from shoulder to knee, bringing back memories of Bible study. She smiled at him, and her soft perfume danced around his nose.

He hadn't counted on the closeness in the pews. Her nearness was both wonderful and painful. But since he was stuck, he might as well enjoy it. One last, grand gesture. That's why he was here.

He started to sling an arm over the back of the pew, but caught himself in time to refrain, though the warmth of her skin, the silky rustle of her dress, the smell of her hair were all balms for his weary, dry spirit.

At some point, the preacher caught his attention and he managed to focus on the sermon.

At first, the minister talked about laying up treasures in Heaven instead of on earth. Drew had no problem at all with that. Too many people were materialistic. But as the preacher expounded on the verses, Drew read farther down the page.

The eye is the lamp of the body. If your eyes are good, your whole body will be full of light. But if your eyes are bad, your whole body will be full of darkness. If then the light within you is darkness, how great is that darkness!

Drew broke out in a sweat. What was this scripture doing in the same chapter with a discussion of materialism? Any talk about eyes upset him. He still hadn't managed an ophthalmologist appointment. What if his eyes went dark forever? What did a blind photographer without a high school education do for a living?

He wondered if God cared one whit about a man's sight and if praying would do any good. Drew was willing to do about anything to save his vision. For himself as well as for Larissa.

He must have made a sound because Larissa turned her head and whispered, "Are you hurting? Do we need to leave?"

Though he wanted to say yes, he shook his head. "I'm good."

Though unconvinced, she returned her attention to the sermon. Drew went back to the disturbing Bible verse. If God was trying to tell him something, he was definitely listening.

After the service, Larissa wanted to take Drew straight home. The stubborn man wouldn't hear of it.

"You're tired," she insisted as they slowly made their way through the foyer and out into the breezy spring day. "Let me take you home."

"I made reservations."

"You did?" She blinked, surprised.

"Yeah, before church, and I'm hungry. Let's go eat."

"You have that pinched look around your mouth."

"More proof that I'm hungry."

"At least let me get the car and drive up closer." The parking lot was huge and Drew had refused to let her drop him off while she parked. His pride had taken enough of a hit when she hadn't let him drive.

This time she should have saved her breath. With dogged determination, Drew set off across the concrete parking lot. Her heels tap-tapped to the rhythm of his thumpety-thump like some bizarre rap tune. If she thought about it much, the combination would make her laugh.

"Where are these secret reservations you've made?" she asked when they were inside the soft leather interior of the Denali.

A tiny smile tipped the corner of his lips. "Riverside Steakhouse."

A sweet memory danced through her head.

"We don't need a reservation there," she said, puzzled. What was going on?

"We do today." Drew kicked the seat back in reclining position and relaxed.

"You *are* tired," she said. "Let me take you home. We can get lunch at a drive-through on our way." As much as she wanted to go to their special restaurant, his health was more important.

He slanted her a look. "I'm good. Just resting the leg. Drive."

"Would you tell me if you were tired?"

"I'm not."

Okay, then, enough of that. "What did you think of church?"

"I thought you were the most beautiful woman there."

"That's not what I asked."

He slipped on his sunglasses, and then rested his head back, eyes closed. From the side, she could see his lashes against his cheek and the supple curve of his mouth and cheekbones. He was a gorgeous man in a rugged, dangerous, purely masculine way. From the turned heads when they'd entered the church this morning, she wasn't the only one who thought so. Or maybe they were curious about the photographer that married one of their own but few had met. His injury in Iraq held a certain fascination for some people.

Whichever, she was proud to have him by her side. She wished he understood that. How proud she was of him, how happy she felt to show him off and call him hers.

They drove along in silence for a while. She thought he was asleep until out of the blue, he said, "I liked your church."

Her mouth curved in a smile. "Does that mean you'll go again sometime?"

"Larissa."

And just like that the sun went behind a cloud.

"You could attend as long as you're here. It wouldn't hurt anything."

He opened his eyes, head swiveling toward her. "Sneaky."

"I've always wanted you beside me at church. I loved having you there."

She sounded pitiful, begging him. Her mother was right. She was pathetic to hang on to a man who didn't want to be with her anymore.

Drew removed the sunglasses. "If it's that important to you."

He didn't look too happy about it, but at least he'd agreed.

Hope bloomed as sweet and lovely as the azaleas in Riverside Park. God was at work. She had to keep believing.

They arrived at the Riverside Steakhouse, a small restaurant along the banks of the Arkansas River running through the beautiful park system of Tulsa. They'd come here to the Riverside many times when they were first married, so his choice of restaurants was no surprise.

As they exited the car, he said, "I wish we could take a walk."

"When your leg is well enough, we'll come back and walk all you want."

Leaning on his crutches, he stopped and stared at her from behind the sunglasses but didn't reply.

The silence spoke volumes. He might be nice enough to make lunch reservations, even go to church with her a couple of times, but he hadn't changed his mind. Only the brokenness of his slowly healing body kept him here now. As soon as he was well, he'd be gone again. He was in Tulsa today because he had no choice. He wouldn't allow her to forget that important fact no matter how unwilling he might be to say the hurtful words.

Sometimes she didn't understand God. He commanded Christians not to divorce, but what did he expect her to do in this awful situation? She'd tossed her pride in the Dumpster and practically begged the man to stay her husband. She didn't know what else to do.

Inside the restaurant the scent of sizzling steaks greeted them.

"I love that smell," she said, and was rewarded with one of Drew's smiles.

On the first night they'd met, he'd brought her here after the gallery showing. They'd sat at a window table overlooking the river, the golden moon reflecting off the water. A band played sixties music, people had laughed and talked, and she'd fallen so in love with Drew she could hardly breathe for the wonder of it.

A pretty young woman in sleek black slacks and pristine white shirt greeted them.

"Mr. Michaels," she said with a curiously bright smile. "Your table is ready."

As the hostess led the way to a very familiar table by the window, an odd feeling shifted through Larissa. She glanced at Drew, but his expression was as bland as buttermilk. Why was he doing this?

Even on crutches he managed to hold her chair, and when his fingers brushed the side of her neck Larissa was sure the touch was accidental. But her insides churned with bewilderment.

"Chocolate truffle mousse cake first or last?" he asked, leaning toward her with that disturbing half-smile. Yes, he was up to something. Drew had always been unpredictable, but she hadn't seen this coming at all.

"First, of course." She smiled, deciding to give in to whatever game Drew had decided to play.

"That's what I figured." He laughed and put in the order, adding their meal and drink orders as well. No sooner had the waitress disappeared than the hostess with the big smile came toward them. This time she carried a bouquet of baby pink roses which she handed to Drew. He nodded his thanks and the hostess left.

"For you," he said.

The same restaurant, the same table, even the same dessert. And now roses. "What is all this, Drew?"

He placed a hand over his heart in mock hurt. "Don't tell me you've forgotten the date."

"Of course I haven't. But…" Tears sprang to her eyes.

Four years ago today they had sat at this very table and fallen in love.

"What are you doing?" she whispered.

"I've made you miserable for months. Let me give you this today, before…" He stopped, leaving the rest unsaid. Before he left for good, he wanted to toss out a few conscience-salving crumbs. She should be angry, but she couldn't muster the strength.

Like the pathetic fool her mother said she was, Larissa wanted to play his game, to pretend just for today that Drew still loved and wanted her.

He took her hand. "Remember how happy we were that night?"

Memories flooded in. "We were crazy."

"You wore a white satiny dress," he said. "And I took so many snapshots of you that I ran out of film."

She pointed out the window. "We walked along the water's edge and almost fell in."

"The night was cold."

"And you kept me warm."

Sadness crept back in for all that they'd had and all that was lost.

"No sad faces." He plucked one of the roses and tickled her arm with it. "Today is special, so we are only going to talk about the good things. Deal?"

There was an almost boyish eagerness in him and Larissa couldn't say no. Truth be told, she didn't want to.

They spent most of the afternoon reminiscing. They talked of their first Christmas. Of the hours spent laughing and kissing while they decorated the gigantic Scotch pine Drew had insisted on buying. They laughed about all the times Larissa had tried and failed to teach Drew the game of golf. About the paint she'd spilled on his head when they redecorated the bedroom. About the afternoon they'd spent in his darkroom, photographs completely forgotten. Of the big things and the little things that made their relationship unique. And special.

Long after their plates were cleared away and coffee was served, they talked. It felt so good to relax and laugh again with Drew. When they'd first married, she'd loved those hours of just talking. Mostly she had talked, but Drew was an amazing listener. He listened as though she was the most fascinating speaker in the world. Once he'd even told her that the sound of her voice was a gift he hid inside. And when he was lonely, he took the sound out and listened to her again.

He could say the most romantic things.

Their relationship had been a dream for a while. And even after they'd begun arguing over his constant travel, making up had been incredible.

"You've proved something to me today, Drew," she said, letting her fingers trail across the back of his hand.

"What's that?"

"What we have is worth saving."

He leaned back in his chair and sighed, a heavy, sad sound. The words brought reality crashing painfully down.

"Some things weren't ever meant to be, Larissa. Our marriage is one of those things."

"You picked a crummy time to decide that."

"I brought you here today because I wanted you to remember the good times, to know how special you are, and to understand that this mess isn't your fault. It's mine."

"But that's the problem. I *don't* understand."

"I know you don't and I can't explain." Drew unfolded the maroon napkin and refolded it again and again. "Just remember that you're an incredible woman who will find a good man in no time and marry again. You won't even remember my name."

"Don't be stupid. You're my husband. The only one I'll ever have. The only one I want."

And then, right there in the restaurant, surrounded by waitstaff and customers, Larissa started to cry.

Something inside Drew broke. "Ah, Larissa. Don't do that. Don't cry."

He felt helpless, out of his element. Give him a tornado or a hurricane, he could deal with that. But seeing Larissa cry, knowing he was the cause, was more torture than a thousand scorpion stings. Like the night of the Bible study, when he'd stood outside the master bedroom, he was lost. Only this time, she was within arm's reach.

Before he could reason things out, he pushed back from the table and had her in his arms. "Don't cry, baby. Don't cry. I'm sorry," he whispered against her hair. "Don't cry."

As he held her, loving her as much as he hated himself, Drew knew one thing for certain.

He was going to regret this.

But right now, he couldn't have cared less.

Chapter Eight

The box arrived on Monday morning.

Drew was in the family room, still chiding himself over Sunday's disaster. He'd expected the lunch to make things easier for her, but he'd only hurt her more. And holding her in his arms had nearly ruined him.

He was a wreck. His insides were as tangled as the pasta salad Larissa was making.

If he didn't get out of here soon, he'd ruin her life forever.

All he could think about was being with her, soaking up every smile, every touch, every moment with her.

And when he lay down at night, his dreams were of her. In every one, she learned the truth about his past and hated him, just as he knew she would in real life.

The doorbell played a happy tune and Larissa went to answer it while he limped into the kitchen. The cast was off but the ankle and heel were going to take more rehab time than he'd hoped. He was sick of the crutches and had decided to tough it out without them from now on.

He had an appointment with an eye doctor next week and with the orthopedist on Friday. Somebody had to get him well fast.

Refrigerator door open, orange juice bottle in one hand, he was about to take a big swig when Larissa came back toting a battered cardboard box.

"It's for you," she said. "From Iraq."

She placed the heavy carton onto the breakfast bar, shooting a warning frown toward his orange juice.

Unrepentant, he grinned and chugged the juice just for the fun of it. After backhanding his mouth, he said, "Probably the stuff I left behind at the base camp. Nice of them to send it."

He scooped the box under one arm and limped to the couch in the family room.

Larissa followed, hovering as if worried that

he'd sprawl onto the tile floor and break something else.

As much as he hated to admit it, he enjoyed the attention. She was as nurturing and fussy as a mother. Not that he knew anything about mothers but Larissa would be a great one. And someday she'd find a man to make her a mommy as many times as she wanted. Someone other than him. His gut clenched at the thought, though he accepted it as the best thing.

He'd been unfair to her from the start about having kids. He should have told her of his conviction that his kind shouldn't reproduce. Like always, he'd only thought of himself and what made him happy instead of her. He hadn't even considered that she would want children.

Now, he was trying to rectify that selfishness, but she refused to cooperate, and he was losing ground fast.

"Do you suppose some of your equipment is in there?"

"I hope so." He'd left a backpack full of extra cameras, films and lenses behind. "I had rolls and rolls of exposed film back at base camp. Some of the shots should be saleable."

A little part of him was terrified that the markets for his work would dry up while he recouped. Another part was terrified that he'd lose his sight and never work again. He needed to get some shots in the pipeline.

Using the scissors Larissa produced from somewhere, he cut and stripped the tape and opened the box. Larissa lifted out a handful of packing to reveal the backpack along with some clothes and personal effects. In the very bottom, carefully wrapped was a dirty, tattered camera.

"Oh, man." He lifted it out, almost reverently.

"What is it?"

"My Nikon. The one I had in my hand when…" He let the sentence drift away. This was the camera he'd had with him during the attack. "I can't believe it survived."

"And that someone salvaged it for you. How very thoughtful."

"Yeah." Camera in hand, he pushed up from the couch. "I have to see what's on here."

His concussed brain had conveniently dumped most of the activities of that last day. Even though he was more than a little afraid to remember, it was time.

"Do you think the film is still good?"

"Only one way to find out."

Since getting the cast off, he'd been able to spend considerable time in the basement darkroom, though all of his photos lately were of the neighbor kids, the dog, the backyard. This collection of film was the real deal, the kind of stuff he lived for. The kind of shots that paid his bills.

Catching his eagerness, Larissa hefted the backpack of equipment and followed him to the stairs. "I worry when you go down these steep steps."

"I like it when you worry about me," he admitted and then wanted to bite his tongue.

She offered a funny look, but said nothing as she flipped on the lights and walked in front of him down the steps in case he stumbled. Instead of the chemical smell of the basement, he caught the scent of her perfume. Like the fool he was, Drew breathed her in.

The windowless lower level was the perfect darkroom, and he'd outfitted it with all the developing equipment he liked best. Over the years of experimenting, he'd developed techniques that gave his work a unique voice in the photography world. This was the place where the magic happened, and he loved being down here.

"Lights off?" Larissa asked when he'd reached the sink and the film tanks.

He nodded. "You're getting pretty good at this."

She smiled and flipped the switch.

Even in the pitch-black room, Drew could feel Larissa moving next to him. Though accustomed to working in the dark by feel, since the accident the lack of light bothered him.

With practiced ease, he quickly went through the motions to protect the precious film and mix the needed chemicals. When he turned the amber safelight on, Larissa had the thermometer and timer at the ready. Since they'd bought this house, he'd been teaching her about the darkroom. She could probably develop this film as well as he could.

Side by side, they worked as a smooth team. He loved spending time with her down here. The darkroom had been a great place to make out.

Better not follow that train of thought.

"Do you remember any of the pictures you took before the accident?" Her voice was hushed.

"My memory is fuzzy of that day, but I know there were some important shots."

"I thought your memory had all come back. Is the concussion still bothering you?" He knew she fretted.

His heart stumbled a little. "Some."

No use lying about it, though his memory was not the brain injury that worried him most.

After what seemed like an eternity of mixing and rotating and dipping and rinsing, ghostly images began to form on the negatives.

"We've got something," he said, excited that the film hadn't been devastated by the blast.

Carefully, Larissa helped him pin the negatives to the line over the sink. One by one, he squinted at the tiny, reversed images, his expert eye seeing the potential in each one.

Suddenly, his heart stopped. "Oh, man."

Larissa, clothespin in hand, rotated toward him. "What?"

He handed her the negative.

She squinted at it. "It's a Middle Eastern man with a huge smile."

Drew's head started to spin. He grabbed for the countertop and leaned forward, all the air going out of him.

"Drew, what in the world is wrong?" Sounding panicked, she rushed to his side. "Who is that?"

He'd forgotten. How could he have forgotten the smiling picture of his driver and friend?

"Amil," he whispered. "It was Amil."

Larissa's stomach quivered with concern. Even in the semi-darkness of the safelight,

Drew's face had drained of all color. She was afraid he might pass out.

Moving close, she slid an arm around his narrow waist. "Are you okay?"

"Yeah. A little dizzy."

"Could I get you something? Some water? Anything?"

He shook his head and took several deep, gulping breaths. "I'm okay. Just shocked for a minute."

Her insides quivered with worry. "Who is Amil?"

"*Was*. Amil was my driver. My buddy. He didn't make it out."

"Oh, Drew. Are you sure?"

"Yeah. I'm sure."

Everything in her ached to wrap her arms around him and pull him close. "I'm so sorry."

"Yeah, me, too. Amil was a good man. I had forgotten about the picture. I snapped it a second before the blast. Seeing his big old friendly smile was quite a shock."

He left the rest unsaid, but Larissa knew what he was thinking. That big old friendly smile was snapped in the last seconds of Amil's life.

She stood next to him, silent, not knowing what to say but also not wanting to move away.

Drew had experienced a horror she couldn't begin to comprehend. She'd never had a friend die before her very eyes. Drew, who was usually so self-contained and independent, needed her comfort and her strength. She just wasn't sure he would accept it.

He straightened from the counter and turned toward her, grief emanating from him like heat waves. She hesitated no longer. She walked into his chest and wrapped her arms around his muscled back. Like a drowning soul, he hugged her close.

They stood together for a long time. He didn't cry. Drew never cried, but she felt his sadness on her like a weight. In the nearly four years of their marriage, she couldn't ever remember a time when he'd leaned on her. The thought made her both sad and glad. She had leaned on him when she was upset, but this was the first time he'd let her share his anguish.

"You know what he said to me right before the blast?" Drew murmured against her ear.

"What?" she asked quietly as she rubbed comforting circles on his back. Still too thin, his backbone bumped against her fingertips.

"He asked me to come to his house and take photos of his family. He was so proud of his children. He talked about them all the time." Another ragged breath ruffled the hair above her ear. "Those kids don't have a dad anymore because he befriended an American photographer."

"You can't blame yourself."

"I don't. I'm just sorry that a family lost a good father and provider. And I lost a friend."

Her heart ached for him. War was ugly. He'd seen his share and then some, but she'd never seen him this affected by the tragedies. He usually kept all his emotions locked inside.

She loosened her hold slightly and tilted back, putting a tiny space between them. "Maybe we could do something for his family."

Drew nodded, thoughtful. "He wanted me to take photos of his sons. Seven of them. I'm going to do that."

And if she knew Drew, he'd do more than take pictures.

"You're a good man, Drew Michaels," she said and without pausing to think, she bracketed his face between her hands and kissed him.

It was meant to be a friendly, comforting kiss, but as soon as their lips met, something inside her snapped.

Drew was her husband, and they'd been apart

both physically and emotionally for a long time. She'd missed him so very, very much.

Apparently, he'd missed her, too, though he'd been saying just the opposite. When she ended the quick, sweet kiss, he pulled her close again.

His lips found hers and the tenderness was such a surprise Larissa melted against him, confused but jubilant. No matter what he said or how many mixed messages he emitted, Drew cared for her.

When the moment ended, he took her hand and led the way to the basement steps.

Once seated side by side, he pressed her hand between both of his. "We need to talk."

She gave a small laugh. "I don't think they call that talking."

One side of his lips quirked upward. "I need to ask you something important."

She went still. He never wanted to talk about really deep issues. "Okay."

"Tell me about your faith. What made you decide to get religious?"

Larissa blinked twice, trying to follow the sudden switch in topics. She'd expected about any question except this, but then, Drew always did the unexpected.

He wanted to discuss her faith. Amazing.

Perhaps God was at work here in the basement of their villa.

"I don't consider it getting religious, exactly," she said carefully, praying all the while. She wanted to say the right things so badly. "I had a religious upbringing, but what I have now is a relationship with Jesus."

"You know I don't understand any of that," he admitted. "I barely know who Jesus is."

"I didn't really know either, but now I do. God so loved the world that He sent His son to die for us. Jesus is that son. And whoever believes in Him will be saved." Nervous that she'd say the wrong things and drive her husband further away, Larissa fidgeted. "See, that's the part that got me. God loved us that much. He doesn't *need* people. He *wants* us, and He was willing to go to extraordinary lengths to win us. I just couldn't resist that kind of love."

Drew's expression grew thoughtful. "What's it like? To be a Christian, I mean."

After coming to Christ, her first desire had been to share her newfound joy with Drew. She wanted him to experience what she had. At the time, he hadn't been interested.

"I'm so new at this, Drew. I don't know a lot

of Bible verses or have many experiences to share, but I know what happened in my heart when I invited Jesus in. One minute everything seemed dark and hopeless. The next it was as if my whole being was filled with light and hope."

"Light and hope," he murmured. "I like the sound of that."

Larissa recognized his longing because she'd been there.

"He'll do the same for you, Drew, if you ask Him."

Absently, he rubbed the side of his healing ankle and stared into the darkened room. "I'll give it some thought."

That was the best she could ask for.

After a moment of silence, he said, "I'm pretty messed up."

"You're mending. Soon, you can get back to work." She tried to sound chipper but the truth depressed. With his body well, he'd no longer have reason to stay.

"I didn't mean physically," he said. "I meant in here." He tapped his chest. "There are things about me you don't know. I doubt God is too interested."

She'd felt the same way before accepting the Lord. "God can fix anything, Drew. No matter how bad we think we've been." She found his hand. "He can even fix our relationship if we'll let Him."

Drew shook his head. "You're amazing, you know that? I don't understand why you're so good to me."

"Then you really are messed up. I love you, you big goof. When we married," she said, "I wanted forever. I planned my life around you, to have a family with you, to grow old together. I can't give up that dream."

The ache and disappointment was there for him to accept or reject. She dug her fingertips into the rough concrete and waited.

"I'm sorry," he said simply. "The one thing I never wanted was to hurt you, and that's all I've ever done."

He was weakening. She was sure of it.

"Not true."

They grew silent and the gentle mood expanded around them. After a bit, Drew pivoted toward her. But as his head swiveled, his eyes widened in fear.

"Drew? What is it? What's wrong?"

He shook his head and scrubbed at his eyes.

A memory pressed at the back of Larissa's mind. She'd witnessed this behavior more than once. And there was the time she'd seen the phone book open to ophthalmologists.

"Is there something wrong with your eyes?"

He blinked over and over again, the bewildered look slowly disappearing.

"Tell me, Drew. What's going on?"

His head dropped. "I didn't want you to know."

She grabbed his wrist. "Know what? What is it? Did something happen that I don't know about?"

"A lot of things happened over there that I never want you to know."

Her stomach started to churn. Her mind raced through the diagnoses various physicians had rendered. None had mentioned anything about his eyes. But she *knew*.

"What's wrong with your vision?"

He blew out a resigned breath. "Okay. You win. You already know about the concussion. What you don't know is that I lost more than a few memories." She heard him swallow. "Sometimes everything goes black."

"What do you mean, *everything?*"

His bleak expression sent fright bumps crawling over her skin.

"Sometimes I lose my vision. At the most unexpected times, it just goes. One minute

I'm seeing, the next a gray fog appears and then the darkness."

"Oh, Drew." She touched the front of his shirt, horrified for him. "Oh, my darling Drew."

He dragged a hand over the aforementioned eyes.

He must be terrified. His eyes were his life.

"What do the doctors say?"

"I don't know."

"Do you mean to tell me that you haven't told your doctor about this?"

"I have an appointment Tuesday."

So that was why the phone book had been open to eye specialists. She moved one step down and turned to look up at him. "When was the last episode?"

"A few days ago while I was playing video pool with Jake." One of the neighborhood kids who found Drew and his camera fascinating company. "The episodes are getting farther apart, so maybe I'm healing."

He didn't sound too convinced. All the times she'd seen him falter and get that odd, frightened look now made sense. "You're scared out of your mind."

A beat of silence and then a gruff admission. "Yeah. What will I do if I lose my vision? I'm a photographer. I can't do anything else."

He was more than scared. He was like a drowning man whose life raft had sprung a leak. She yanked his hands into hers and gave them a shake.

"You listen to me, Drew Michaels. You are not going to lose your eyesight. We'll get help. And we'll pray. I'll have my entire church pray."

God wouldn't let this happen, would he?

Drew pulled back a little, shaking his head. "I don't want anyone to know. I don't want pity."

Which was probably why he'd chosen to carry this awful secret alone.

"That's too bad. Sometimes you need people, Drew. Right now, we need doctors and we need prayer warriors." She levered up on her knees and leaned toward him. "You're a fighter. I'm a fighter. Together, with God's help, we will find an answer."

Very slowly Drew began to relax. His worried frown eased away and a tiny smile dawned. Her faith and love had given him hope.

"You know, Larissa," he said softly, "if you keep this up, I'm going to start believing in the impossible."

"Nothing, *nothing* is impossible," she said.

And then she kissed him. Hard. He laughed, the maniac. Then she laughed, too. The man had just told her he might be losing his eyesight and they were both sitting in the dark basement laughing.

And she actually felt more hope at this moment than she'd felt in months.

Chapter Nine

Drew sat on the edge of the backyard hot tub, contemplating the mysteries of the universe. Or rather, the mysteries of his beautiful wife.

Coco, the chipper little Yorkie, listened to his mutterings with an attentive ear.

The conversation in the darkroom had changed things between him and Larissa. Well, the conversation and the kiss. He couldn't get the sweetness out of his mind.

Why had she kissed him? Out of pity for the vision problem? Or because she loved him even if he was going blind?

She confused him. Or maybe he confused himself. Either way, his insides swirled and spun like the hot tub.

For all her quiet grace, Larissa was a tiger for

the underdog and right now, that was him. He found it next to impossible to resist her. In fact, he'd almost given up trying. As long as she was in close proximity, he didn't stand a chance against her constant barrage of unfailing love and support. Resistance would have to take a back burner until he could put distance between them.

Right now, Larissa was love in action. Nobody could resist that.

During the last week she had dragged him from doctor to doctor, she'd researched on the Internet, she'd called in her "prayer warriors." None of the specialists had a definitive answer for his visual disturbances, but Larissa subscribed to the proposition that a mix of concussion and mental trauma was the culprit.

Either sounded good to him. He could control his mind and the concussion would heal. He hoped. Other than a couple of incidents of blurriness this week, he'd experienced no total darkness.

Telling Larissa had taken the edge off his fear. Still, he wanted to memorize the world around him, just in case the worst happened. For a man who lived for color and light, the thought that those might disappear forever shook him to the core.

"What would I do, Coco? Not much market for a blind photographer."

Coco jammed a comforting head beneath his hand. Drew stroked the soft, silky fur.

"You look silly with red toenails," he said affectionately. Larissa had the little dog groomed weekly, a waste of time and money, but Coco always smelled good. Not as good as Larissa, of course.

Feet hanging in the swirling waters of the hot tub, he rotated the ankle as the physical therapist had taught him and wrote the alphabet with his toes. He was getting better, stronger. Another week or two.

And then what?

Steam drifted up around him. The air outside was cool with a touch of breeze. He was tempted to slide his whole body into the hot tub, khaki shorts and all.

In his previous times at home, he'd been raring to leave after a few weeks. Now he felt a strange reluctance, as if leaving would be the end of him.

Maybe it would be.

"Would you miss me, Coco?" He'd miss her. He'd miss this house and the grounds. He'd miss the convenience of his own personal darkroom.

Most of all, he'd miss his wife.

Blowing out an exasperated sound, he dragged a hand over his scratchy whiskers.

"God, if you're up there, help me do the right thing for once in my rotten life."

The right thing, to his way of thinking, was still to let her go, let her find someone who could give her all the good things she deserved. But lately, he was weakening. He was tempted to call the whole divorce thing off, to beg forgiveness, and promise Larissa the world. But he knew better than to go that route. When he made a promise, he kept it. Trouble was, he couldn't promise what she wanted, and he would never lie to her. Never. She was the one thing in his life that was clean and pure and devoid of deceit. He might not tell her everything but he had never lied to her either.

Maybe they could find a compromise. But what kind of compromise could a man offer to a woman who wanted nothing but him and his babies.

He kicked out with his injured foot and splashed his own face.

If he lost his vision, he couldn't even support her or himself. He would be nothing but a parasite.

Beyond photography he had no talents. His repertoire of skills consisted of stealing, fighting and lying, all honed at an early age, but now lying dormant and rusty. As angry as he'd been back then, the fire had served up a warning he'd heeded. With his new identity, he'd shed the troubled skin of teenage Drew Grace in exchange for manhood and a career. He wasn't that person anymore. But the wasted years had left him with nothing worthwhile to fall back on.

"Beyond photography and playing video games, I'm pretty useless," he said to Coco. The dog sidled up closer and grinned, tail wagging. "Oh, yeah and I'm a pretty good ear scratcher."

The dog writhed in ecstasy while he proved the point.

"She loves me, Coco." Coco cocked her head and offered a puzzled frown. "Yeah, I wonder the same thing. Why would an incredible woman like Larissa marry a messed-up dude like me in the first place?"

No sensible reason at all.

"I don't know why, but she does. I feel it." He tapped his chest. "In here. Don't tell anyone, but I love her, too."

She was the only human being in his entire adulthood who had said those words to him. All week, he had felt the power of her love as she'd hounded doctors and encouraged him to keep believing.

He'd given God a lot of thought lately, too. Was Larissa right? Could God fix a messed-up man with so much hidden baggage that he could barely sleep at night?

He had a hard time believing that anyone or anything could erase the tragedies of his past. What was done could not be undone. And yet, he wanted to believe that God could take away the awful guilt.

He sucked in a lungful of moist, heated air, then exhaled very slowly.

He'd never before understood what people got out of religion, but Larissa's explanation of light and dark made perfect sense to a photographer. And the strange scripture from church was starting to make sense, too. Deep down, something was missing inside him. He'd always thought it was a soul, an empty hole brought about by never belonging anywhere or to anyone. Never feeling loved. He'd been such an angry kid and once the anger was under control, he'd filled the void with work. That's what a therapist had once said, but now he wondered. Was the empty place waiting to be filled with the light of God?

It was a topic worthy of serious consideration.

Kids' laughter drifted over the privacy fence. Drew shook his head and laughed with them. The gang must be on the way to entertain him for the afternoon. Weird that he actually looked forward to a bunch of rug rats invading his space.

Larissa stepped out onto the patio. His stomach went south and flip-flopped like a banked koi.

"Your agent called."

He still got a weird rush at the idea of hiring an agent. The last thing he'd ever desired was public notice, given the secret past that could send him to prison. But somehow his photos had taken on a life of their own. He'd wound up with an agent who arranged to have his work hung in galleries and displayed for the art connoisseur to covet. The real work of photo assignments he handled for himself. He'd only hired the agent so he wouldn't have to think about business too much.

Hanging out with rich crowds was a different matter altogether. He hated that part, although his presence at some gatherings was occasionally required. Or so declared his hyper-active agent, Shelby Kates.

"What did she want?" he groused as Larissa swung toward him in a pair of green capris and a fitted blouse that showed off her curves to perfection. His beautiful wife was another reason he didn't want to go blind. He raised his camera and pushed the shutter. She was so ac-customed to his constant snapping that she didn't even react.

"Call her back. Something about a showing." She tossed him a fluffy towel that smelled of fabric softener. "Mother will be here soon. Better put on a shirt."

"Great." He made a face, then dried his feet and limped to the phone.

A couple of kids he'd never seen in his life pushed open the French doors. One was a tall, lanky teenage boy with a pearl in his upper lip and a tattoo on his earlobe.

Shaking his head at his wife's eclectic mix of friends, Drew called his agent and discovered he was expected in Charleston on Saturday evening.

Saturday. He'd promised to attend church again on Sunday morning, but Larissa would understand. Duty called.

Soon, the real duty would be calling. What

would happen then? Would he follow through with his original plan? Could he?

Right now, he wasn't even sure he could handle a weekend showing. Though his stamina was gradually returning, he couldn't be on the ankle any time without it swelling to the size of a basketball. Most of all, he had a horror of going blind in public.

With a shiver of apprehension, he went to find Larissa and break the news. Before he could, Marsha Stone breezed into his house carrying a stack of decorator portfolios.

"Larissa, darling," she called. The woman hadn't even knocked.

Marsha spotted him. Mouth drawn up as if she smelled a skunk, she was the picture of disapproval. He raised one hand. "Excuse me. I'll find a shirt."

Anything to keep Marsha off Larissa's case. But this was his house and if he wanted to run around without a shirt, he should be able to.

The thought stopped him cold. He'd called this *his house,* not just Larissa's.

Whoa. He really *was* getting too comfortable.

By the time he'd dressed in a pair of familiar old jeans and a time-softened chambray shirt, Larissa and her mother had samples of wallpaper and paint spread all over the family room. Marsha, it seemed, was redecorating again. This was an election year and with Larissa's dad up for reelection, they would do a great deal of entertaining.

The whole idea made Drew tired, primarily because he knew Larissa would end up with the bulk of the work. The effort would be too much for Marsha and his kindhearted wife would never complain. She would just shoulder the load and make her mother happy. She was too good for all of them.

As a diversion from the redecorating schemes, he spent the morning in the darkroom explaining the pros and cons of various chemical mixes to the skinny teenager. Ryan, lip ring and all, turned out to be a camera buff and one of Larissa's tenderhearted attempts to fix the world. More importantly, to Drew anyway, he was a foster kid living with the Ratcliffs down the street.

That alone was enough to get his sympathy.

The boy was interested in photography and filmmaking but not much else.

To tell the truth, the kid kind of reminded Drew of himself back at the beginning when he'd taken that first newspaper job. Only fifteen, he'd lied, claimed to be eighteen, and by the time he needed proof, he'd been on the streets long enough to buy a counterfeit birth certificate, complete with new name, new birth date, and an acceptable, though altogether fake set of parents.

That first job had changed his life. No longer a runaway foster kid, he had learned the fundamentals of photography from a patient veteran.

Ryan displayed a similar intensity when looking through a camera, and Drew found that hard to resist. The kid knew more about digital photography and software than Drew ever wanted to know. To him, photographs were born wet, not inside a computer. The whole digital business, in his opinion, stole the credibility of the work. He'd used the method when time and distance were an issue, but in the end he always returned to the darkroom. In his view and that of other old-school photographers, there was something far more mysterious and artistic and challenging in capturing the perfect shot on site. Digital manipulation seemed like cheating to him.

But he didn't tell the kid that. Not today anyway. He *did* tell him the truth though when the boy lamented his lousy cheap camera. Cameras don't take pictures. Photographers do.

And he proved the point by taking Ryan and his lousy cheap camera to Riverside Park for a lesson in light and patience and awaiting the perfect shot.

At noon, he bought the teen a burger and dropped him off at the Ratcliffs' place. Poor joker was stuck in tutoring during spring break after failing ninth grade English. School was one place Drew couldn't offer any assistance. He'd never finished ninth grade English.

"Tomorrow?" Ryan had asked hopefully.

"Sure. Or better yet, show up here about an hour before sunset tonight. We'll have a little fun with color."

The lanky boy hitched one shoulder as if he really didn't care one way or the other, but Drew caught the glint in his eyes. He'd show up.

Back at the house, Marsha was thankfully gone. Larissa had a telephone jammed between shoulder and ear while she scribbled madly on a yellow tablet. She gave him a quick smile that did funny things to his chest. He winked and took her picture. She turned her back and waved him away.

His leg was killing him, but he faked a straight walk to the bedroom, changed into swim trunks and T-shirt, then headed for the hot tub. The heated, churning water gave him more relief than Lortab and left his head a lot less fuzzy.

"Are you out here again?" Larissa called from the back door.

"Why don't you join me?"

The French doors banged shut.

He grinned. Maybe he shouldn't have said that.

With a press of a button, he activated the stereo system. Rascal Flats was singing about a broken road. He could relate. He'd been down a few of those.

The March wind was chilly, an interesting contrast to the steamy tub. Resting his head back in the indention, he floated, letting the ache of standing too long at the park seep out into the water and wishing he knew how to fix the broken road he was on right now.

From the doorway, Larissa watched Drew sleep. Coco lay like a tiny lion on the ledge of the tub, watching, too.

In repose, Drew looked boyish and vulnerable. More than once in their relationship she'd wondered what he'd been like as a child. The dabs of information he'd shared gave her some insight, but she was sad to know all his childhood photos had been lost in the tragic fire that stole his family. He must have been a handsome little boy.

If they had a son, would he look like Drew?

The thought shot an arrow of sorrow into her heart. What if Drew divorced her? What if they never had a child together? Even though he ran scared every time she'd mentioned having a baby, she hadn't given up the dream. Maybe she was a fool and would end up with a broken heart and a broken marriage, but she couldn't stop praying for her husband. Since the day in the basement, he'd become more approachable, less cantankerous, more like the man she'd married. And she had grabbed on to hope with both hands and hadn't let go.

Now here she was standing at the back door staring out at her husband with love and longing.

She'd been watching him a lot lately. Watching him with the neighbor kids, with the dog, with his painstaking perfection in his work, even with her petulant mother. Today she'd admired the patience and respect he had displayed with the troubled Ryan, although from the looks of him, the outing had cost him physically.

Not that he'd ever admit the pain.

There was much about Drew Michaels to

admire. Had she ever expressed that to him? Had she ever told him that he was an amazing man with many good qualities? Or had she, as she feared, been too focused on her own agenda for their relationship to let her husband know how special and important he was?

He'd suffered so many hurts and losses, not the least of which was the death of his family. And now the fear of losing his vision hovered over him like a vulture. He'd once confided that he'd learned his trade on the fly, not in college. Yet, he'd risen to the top of his field.

Yes, Drew Michaels was a unique and gifted man, and she was proud to call him husband.

Earlier today, she'd tried talking to her mother, hoping for some advice in mending the troubled relationship. She should have saved her breath.

Seated side by side with a wallpaper book between them, trying to choose between stripes or floral, all Mother had done was offer for the third time to pay for a divorce. Regardless that Larissa loved the man and never mind that her faith did not allow divorce, her parents thought they knew best.

"It's very clear to everyone that Drew has no

intention of ever being a real husband," her mother had said. "If you want a family and a decent man, you have to get a divorce now. You aren't getting any younger, you know."

That little dig had hurt, as it always did.

Now as she gazed out at her husband, heart filled with emotion, Larissa still thought her parents were wrong. Marriage was worth fighting for. God ordained it and she believed it.

With her stomach jumping like a bunch of puppies, she quietly opened the back door and went to join Drew.

He didn't stir at her approach so she sat quietly on the opposite side and enjoyed the view. Coco raised a golden eyebrow in question but didn't move.

Larissa was tempted to snap Drew's photo for a change, but even in sleep, he kept one hand around the camera.

Monarch butterflies flitted among the blooming azalea bushes, a regular stop on their migration route.

Somewhere in the neighborhood a car door slammed and over the hum and slosh of the hot tub motor, she heard the bounce of a driveway basketball game. All her usual visitors had taken off for other interests the minute her mother had appeared, but she figured some would return later.

She dangled her feet in the water, wishing Drew would wake up. She kicked a little. He slept on.

She kicked a wider arc. Still no response.

Finally, orneriness took hold and she flipped a handful of water in his face.

He awakened with a roar. Before Larissa could think or act, Drew heaved his tall, thin but muscular form across the width of the tub and grabbed her feet. Orneriness flashed in dark, gleaming eyes.

Coco leaped to her feet and barked like a Doberman.

Larissa squealed. "Don't you dare. I mean it, Drew."

Of course, that was the wrong thing to say. With a wicked grin, he yanked her heels. Clothes and all, she plunged into the water. The sudden heat stole her breath. She fought to gain her feet but just that quick, two strong arms swooped her up. She emerged spluttering.

Drew was laughing. "How's the water?"

"Hot." She slapped a handful at him.

He dodged to one side and laughed more.

"Could be why they call it a hot tub."

"Har-har. Very funny." She let her body buoy

up and down in the deep water. Already wet, she might as well enjoy the therapy. "I came out here to talk to you about something."

Whether he wanted to hear it or not, she was going to tell him straight out.

"Good. I have a couple of things to discuss with you as well." He guided her back against the side and stood facing her.

Floating easily, she draped both arms over the outside of the tub as an anchor. "Is this about the call from your agent?"

"Some of my work is being shown in Charleston next weekend. She thinks I need to be there."

She didn't like the sound of that. He hadn't been any farther than downtown Tulsa since the accident, and that exhausted him. "Are you physically ready for a trip like that?"

"I don't know."

"Then, there's your answer. You can't go."

"It's an important opportunity," he said. "I can't pass it up. Especially now that…" He let the thought trail away, but Larissa intuitively caught his meaning.

"Your vision worries me, too. What if—"

"Yeah," he interrupted. Gazing off in the distance, he dipped a hand into the water and slicked back his hair. "What if I suddenly go blind in a strange airport?"

As if startled to have spoken the fear aloud, he faked a grin and tapped her on the chin. "Never mind. I'll be okay."

She caught his hand and gave it a shake. Water sluiced up and around them. "You're not going alone, Drew. I'm going with you."

His heart thumped once, hard, against his rib cage. "I can't ask you to do that."

"You didn't. I offered. And it's a great idea, even if I do say so myself. I've never been to Charleston, and they say it's a wonderful city."

Yeah, wonderfully romantic. And Larissa was warming to the idea.

Giving her fingers a squeeze, he shook his head. "I don't know, 'Rissa."

"The beach, the history, dinner cruise ships." She lit up with excitement. "Come on, Drew. We'll make it fun. What do you say?"

He wanted to say she was scaring him to death. He wanted to say that a weekend in a romantic city with his beautiful wife sounded incredible. He wanted to say he loved her.

Instead he tried to back off a little to arrange a business deal. "Would you really do that? Go as my Seeing Eye person?"

A little of her excitement dimmed. "No."

But then she smiled, slow and sweet, and Drew knew he was in trouble. She knew exactly what he was up to.

"I will not be your Seeing Eye *person*, Drew. I'm your *wife*, your helpmate, like the Bible says. When one of us is weak, the other is strong. That's what marriage is. That's what I want to be. That's what I am."

He stood staring into violet eyes filled with love he didn't deserve and thought his heart might come out of his chest. "I don't understand you at all."

"Okay, then. Let me be very blunt." She swallowed, a nervous action that belied her assertive words. She was afraid of his reaction, but willing to take a chance, a fact that threatened Drew's resolve in the worst way. "I love you, Drew, more this moment than ever before. I've loved you since the first time I laid eyes on you. And I'm not ever going to stop. No matter what you do or say, I will never, ever stop loving you."

Drew closed his eyes against the blast of pure love flowing from her to him. And along with love came a hope shining brighter than the morning sun over Hawaii.

He was a jerk of the first order, but even he

couldn't say no this time. As hard as he'd fought to keep his distance, he wasn't strong enough to battle a force as strong as Larissa's love.

God above knew this was the wrong thing to do, but Drew was lost.

"Ah, 'Rissa," he groaned, barely recognizing his own agonized voice.

She touched him then, pressing fingertips against his lips. "Ssh. It will be wonderful, Drew. A chance to make things right, like a second honeymoon. Please, let all this other stuff go, whatever was wrong, and let's be happy again."

The last sentence ruined him. He was done for. He had the power to make his beautiful wife happy for a few days. He had to do it. And as selfish as he was, he wanted one more special memory to cherish. They'd go to Charleston, he'd do everything in his power to give her an amazing time and make her happy.

In the back of his mind, he knew it would never be enough. Whether today, or next week, or three years from now, Larissa would one day wake up and see him as the worst mistake she'd ever made.

But for now, he'd selfishly take whatever she offered.

Chapter Ten

The atmosphere in the gallery was posh. Attending patrons were old Southern money with blue blood flowing back to the Civil War. They spoke in low modulated murmurs, the gentle lilt of South Carolina a real pleasure to listen to. A group of well-dressed men had retired to the outer balcony to smoke cigars and drink something a bit more potent than punch. Briefly, Drew wished to join them, but he couldn't of course, being the center of attention. And he knew Larissa didn't approve or partake.

At present, he held the rapt attention of an attractive woman along with an art reviewer, both of whom eyed him with something other than artistic interest.

Where was Larissa anyway? Or his agent?

Someone needed to rescue him from magazine writers and overzealous ladies with big bank accounts.

In truth, reviewers scared him spitless. What if they delved too deeply into his background? In the back of his mind was the constant terror that his crime would be discovered.

Another reason he shouldn't have given in to Larissa. He'd ignored the most important reason why he had to let her go.

He glanced around, caught a glimpse of his lovely wife making polite conversation with a guy in a tuxedo. She looked stunning as always, and he wondered again why she'd chosen him. That was his wife over there. The most feminine, elegant woman in the room. Her dress and jewelry were understated, her hairstyle simple, and her makeup light. She fit in with these people in a way that he never could, but she loved *him*.

Unbelievable.

He smiled. How could he expect to fit in when he was the only man in the place not wearing a suit?

Getting dressed in the hotel room tonight had been sensory overload. Even now, her soft fragrance and velvet skin lingered in his mind like a love song.

So far, his vision had been fine, but Larissa watched him carefully, never getting too far away.

This second honeymoon idea of hers was more difficult than he'd imagined. Not because he wasn't having a great time. But because he was. Maybe it was the beautiful city or the Southern charm, but here Larissa made him forget all the reasons they were wrong for each other.

Here in Charleston, everything was right.

"Drew," an ultrafeminine Southern voice murmured.

He'd zoned out for a minute and totally missed the woman's question.

"Sorry. My mind strayed." Shelby had threatened to choke him if he was rude to anyone tonight. But with Larissa on his mind, no one else much mattered. They were having a great time and he wanted to soak up every single minute.

"Excuse me," he said as politely as possible. "I need to go find my wife."

Larissa saw her husband slicing through the press of people like a lone wolf whose attention was riveted on his prey. His noticeable limp somehow made him ever more ruggedly attractive.

Pure delight zipped through her veins.

He was coming for her.

Thank goodness.

In thirty seconds flat, he was beside her.

"Excuse us, please," he said to her companion, and then without further explanation, one hand around her upper arm, moved them toward the door.

"What are you doing?" she whispered.

White teeth flashed. "Kidnapping my wife."

"You can't just leave."

"Watch me."

"Drew, there are people in there spending good money for your autographed prints."

"And I appreciate them." One hand to the small of her back, he guided her rapidly down the hall toward the elevators. Once inside, he breathed a loud sigh of relief. "I couldn't take it anymore. When I saw that guy talking to you with that lecherous grin on his face, that was it."

"He wasn't lecherous. Just boring."

"I'm a man. I know lecherous."

She giggled. "I think you were jealous."

"You'd think right." He backed her against the mirrored wall and kissed her. "I'd rather hang out with you than all the checkbooks in Charleston."

Larissa's insides did a happy dance. When

he'd finally agreed to this trip, he'd thrown himself wholeheartedly into it. She could scarcely believe this was the same brooding, cranky man who claimed to want a divorce.

Though he'd not said anything, she was almost sure he'd changed his mind. God's word was true. Her steadfast love had won him back. Love hadn't failed.

"Where are we going?" she asked with a smile.

He quirked a teasing eyebrow. "Anywhere but here."

Like two sneaking kids, they hurried out of the gallery. Once outside, Drew grabbed her hand and started to run.

"Drew, you're going to hurt your leg!"

Indeed, he was limping badly, but he didn't let up. She caught his spirit of fun and, in spite of her fitted dress and heels, she ran, too.

By the time they reached the beachfront, they were both breathless and laughing.

"You are crazy," she said when she could breathe again.

The only natural light was a flat white moon, but the condos and hotels above the shoreline illuminated the sand-strewn beach enough for walking. Too early in the season for the usual crush of tourists, the beach was all but deserted.

Farther down, she spotted two other couples and a family with a large dog, but their piece of the ocean was romantically empty.

They removed their shoes and strolled. "This place is so beautiful."

A few dinner boats were out on the water. The surf sloshed and pulsed against the shore.

Drew pointed in the distance at a huge light revolving against the night sky. "Don't see too many lighthouses in Oklahoma."

They both grinned at the silly idea of a lighthouse in the landlocked state.

"There's a dock up farther, I think. Want to go sit and make out?"

Larissa bopped him playfully. "I think *you're* the lecher."

"Okay." He sighed in mock defeat. "We can sit and *talk*."

The wooden boards of the dock echoed beneath their bare feet. They walked to the end and sat, dangling their legs over the edge.

"You don't think a shark will jump up and grab my foot, do you?" Larissa asked, wiggling her hot-pink toenail.

"Are you afraid of some poor little shark?"

"I'm a landlubber. Sharks and big water scare me."

Drew draped an arm around her shoulders and pulled her next to his side. He was warm and solid.

"You're safe with me, darlin'," he said, and Larissa believed that with all her heart. Drew would protect her from anything.

Anything but himself.

They sat for a while, heads touching, as they stared into the vast, black ocean. There was something surreal about sitting in the darkness with the man she loved, the sound of the ocean alive around them.

After a while, Drew said, "Have you ever been to Alaska?"

"No. Why?" Please don't say you're about to run off there on some assignment.

"I'd like to take you there someday," he said, and the words were music to her ears. "The water is so blue and the land still pristine. On nights like this, you can sometimes see the northern lights."

"I remember the pictures you took. Incredible."

"Yeah. I waited for weeks to get those exact shots, waiting for the colors." He chuckled softly. "Do you know how cold a man can get sitting for hours in the dark in Alaska?"

"And you want to take me there?" she asked in pretend horror.

"Ulterior motive. You could keep me warm."

"Oh, you." She bumped his side with her shoulder.

"Ouch. Watch out for the ribs."

"I thought they were healed."

"They are."

She made a face at him.

"I'm glad we came here," he said.

"To the beach?"

The breeze tossed her hair into her eyes. Drew brushed it back, carefully looping it behind her ears. He loved touching her. "I meant to Charleston."

"Me, too," she murmured. "I'm happy, Drew. You make me happy."

The statement both pleased and frightened. Was it possible that they could make this work? That he could change and be the man she wanted?

He wanted to, with all his heart and soul. He'd even told her he would try to stay home more. As long as no one discovered his past, they'd be okay. He had to try, for her sake.

"What did your mother say about us coming here together?" Her parents were going to be livid to know the marriage they'd tried to sabotage was once again gaining ground.

"Oh, you know Mother. She was worried

about who was going to help her with the paint contractors while I'm gone."

She hadn't exactly answered his question, but knowing Marsha, the paint contractors *were* more important than her daughter's marriage. Especially since she and Thomas were certain the marriage was dead. Drew had never told Larissa about the time the honorable senator had offered him a lot of money to get lost for good.

"Did you tell your dad?"

"Mother will tell him, I'm sure." She touched his cheek. "Let's not talk about them. Tonight is about us."

The mention of her parents and their ongoing disapproval of him as a husband put a momentary damper on the night.

"Sorry. I promised only happy talk this weekend." He stroked a finger down her forehead, over her nose, and stopped at her lips.

She caught his fingertip between her teeth and nipped gently.

"Ouch." Playfully, he shook the hand as though a shark had bitten him.

"Tell me about your dreams, Drew," she said, with a bemused smile. "What do you see in the future that excites you?"

"The Amazon," he answered without hesitation.

She tilted her head. "The Amazon? I thought you'd been there."

"There are places in the forest that modern man has never seen. I dream of getting those first shots."

He didn't want to think about the other things he dreamed about. He wished he could find his brothers. He wished he could understand God and all the injustices of life better. And he wished he could be the man Larissa deserved.

But he kept all those dreams to himself. Some things were too hard to talk about.

"What about you? What do you dream of, Larissa?"

"Easy one. You and me."

"I like the sound of that." He moved to kiss her, but she stopped him with a hand to his lips.

"Let me finish."

Her soft, luminous eyes were so serious, butterflies invaded Drew's chest. "Okay."

"I dream of you and me—" she hesitated for a nanosecond and then rocked his world "—having a baby."

Everything in him went still. A moment ago he was prepared to kiss her. Now he wanted to run, bad leg and all. Adrenaline shot through his blood vessels and into his brain. His insides started to shake.

Larissa must have felt his reaction because she yanked away.

He reached for her. "Larissa. Honey."

"Don't, Drew. You asked me about my dreams and then you throw them back at me. I want to have a family." Her voice trembled. "That's a perfectly normal dream."

Panic crept up his back and camped on his shoulder. "Before we married you never said anything about wanting kids."

"Everyone wants kids. Why would we have to discuss something so fundamental?"

"Look." At a loss, he stared down at his hands. Telling the truth was impossible. "There are some things a man just knows about himself."

"And you're convinced that you can't be a good father."

"Yeah."

"Drew, that's crazy. Why would you think such a thing?"

The adrenaline shakes grew worse. His mouth was drier than sand. "I've never been around kids. I know nothing about them."

True enough. He never wanted her to know

the rest. That he'd come from the bottom of the barrel. From a family so dysfunctional that he'd ended up on the streets without a clue where his mother was or even who his father might be. Dysfunction was in the blood, and he wasn't about to pass it on to some innocent little baby.

They both fell silent, lost in thought. A cruise ship motored past a few hundred yards offshore.

He'd done it again. While trying to make her happy, he'd made her sad.

When Larissa spoke, her voice was soft and tremulous. "You're wonderful with the neighbor kids." The sentiment touched him. The plea nearly killed him. "Will you at least give it some consideration?" She reached out a hand in a gesture of peace. "Please."

Total mush, what else could he do?

"Sure, babe, sure," he murmured, taking her soft hand in his. "I'll think about it."

Late that night, long after Larissa's soft breathing filled the hotel room, Drew sat on the side of the bed fully dressed. He was thinking about it all right. He couldn't think of anything else.

Head in his hands, he pondered what to do. Larissa made him vulnerable in a way that scared him out of his mind. He was well enough to get back to work. He'd even told Shelby tonight to pass the word around to the right people. At the moment his agent wasn't all that happy with him for abandoning the party, but she was a trooper. She'd be okay.

Larissa stirred behind him, mumbling something in her sleep. He didn't turn to look at her. He was dying inside. Looking at her asleep would finish him off.

Maybe he'd make a few calls when they returned to Tulsa, see what he could get going. He'd hoped to photograph the mysterious purple glow that only appeared at sunset after a volcanic eruption. If he hurried, before the atmosphere in Indonesia cleared, there might still be time.

A baby. He gripped the front of his hair with both hands and pulled. He couldn't be a father. He didn't know how.

Larissa would make a great mother.

"Oh, God," he breathed into the darkness, and just like that he found himself praying. Larissa put a lot of stock in prayer and church and all that. Maybe God would change her mind, make her see reason. God knew Drew's background and his shortcomings far better than Larissa ever would. "She'll listen to You. Make her see what a dumb idea this is."

He didn't know what he expected but nothing happened.

He tried again.

"Okay, God. I don't know much about You, but I'd like to. For Larissa's sake. It would mean a lot to her. Maybe You could help me out here."

Still nothing. He wondered if there was some kind of password or something that Christians used to get God's attention. To let God know the prayer was from a believer. Maybe that's why God didn't answer. Drew had never been an atheist, but he didn't have what his wife had either. She shone with an inner light that hadn't been there before.

He, on the other hand, was about as dark inside as an arctic winter.

What did it take for a man to find that light? Church? Prayer? He'd tried both.

The little fish around his neck claimed that God would never leave or forsake him.

"Then why don't You answer me? Why have I never felt Your presence the way Larissa claims to?"

The walls were silent. In the adjacent suite someone flushed a toilet.

Drew shook his head.

Feeling like a fool for talking to the darkness, he rose and went into the bathroom.

It was going to be a very long night.

Chapter Eleven

Larissa hummed a popular praise song as she crossed the parking lot and entered the tasteful reception area of her father's office. God was good. Life was good. She had so much to be thankful for, and on this glorious, sunny Monday morning gratitude overflowed.

The trip to Charleston had been wonderful. Other than the one dark moment when they'd argued, the few days of R & R had revived their relationship. Drew had shown her in a thousand ways that he loved her. They'd had so much fun sightseeing. They'd spent hours talking until she knew her husband better than ever before. And best of all, Drew had promised to consider having a baby.

Please, dear Lord, bring him around to my way of thinking. I want a baby so badly.

She'd left him piddling with chemicals in the darkroom and fully expected to see a new batch of beach photos when she arrived home.

"Hi, Cynthia," she said to the receptionist. "My dad is expecting me."

"You look really chipper this morning," Cynthia said with a smile.

"I am. I had a great mini-vacation to Charleston."

"Lucky you." The receptionist waved toward the inner office. "Go on through. There's nobody with him right now."

Lucky? she thought as she pushed the door open into her father's office. No, not lucky. Larissa didn't believe that way anymore. She believed the Lord had blessed her because she hadn't given up on her marriage during a time when it would have been easier to quit than to stand and fight. She'd followed the Lord's guidance and He hadn't let her down.

Her father, State Senator Thomas Stone, rose from behind a long executive desk, buttoning his suit jacket out of long habit. He was ever the politician, even with his family.

"Larissa, sweetheart."

Larissa hurried around the desk for a hug. Wrapped in the familiar bulk of her father, she leaned for a moment, drawing in the warmth and security of his embrace. As a child, and continuing into adulthood, Dad had been her rock. Even though he strongly disapproved of Drew, he was still her dad.

"How's my girl?"

"Couldn't be better." She pecked him on the cheek and circled back around the desk to a chair.

"Good. It's time to get serious about our strategy, our media blitz, town hall meetings." He reseated himself, automatically undoing the button over his generous middle. "You're the best strategist on the team."

"You always say that, but it's your indefatigable honesty and hard work that keep the voters coming back."

"This year's fight on Internet controls may give us some trouble. My opponent is adamantly against censorship of any kind."

"But you're leading the battle against child porn, Dad. The voters know how important it is to protect our most innocent citizens." She was proud to have a father of such integrity.

"Yes, they do, but everyone has a different

idea about how to make that happen. It's a very hot topic."

"Along with a dozen others you face all the time." She grabbed a notepad and scribbled some thoughts. "I already have some ideas on this, but Elbert will likely know which direction to take." Elbert was their campaign manager. "Do you want to use that new local company for our campaign ads this time?"

"Stop just a minute, Larissa."

She blinked up at him.

"I didn't ask you here today to work on the campaign."

She laid the pen and pad back on his desk. "You didn't?"

"No." Her father shifted in the leather executive chair, suddenly looking uncomfortable. "We need to discuss something."

Oh. Now she knew. She sat back.

"Mother must have told you about Drew and me getting back together." If she were a porcupine, her quills would be quivering.

"Yes."

Before he could list all the reasons why she should go through with the divorce, Larissa rushed to defend her marriage.

"Dad, I made a vow before God. Drew is my

husband. We're working things out. I love him. Can't you be happy for us?"

Blue eyes never leaving her face, her father fidgeted with a fine ballpoint pen. "Your happiness is all I've ever wanted."

She softened. "I know, Daddy. And I *am* happy. With Drew."

"When this divorce issue first came up, I did something that may upset you. Please believe me when I say I had your best interests at heart. Still do. I simply thought you might need some ammunition."

"Ammunition? For what?" He made her marriage sound like a battle zone. It had never been that.

"You stand to lose a great deal if Drew decided to fight you in court."

"A great deal of money, you mean." Didn't he understand that there was much more at stake here than money? There was her life and her heart.

"Your trust fund is not something to lightly dismiss, Larissa. Men have married women for far less."

Dread and anger pushed at the back of her eyelids. How dare her father insinuate that Drew was after her money!

"Daddy, I can't believe you said that. I can't believe you think I'm that foolish."

"You're not foolish at all. But you are young and trusting."

She laughed bitterly. "I'm not all that young either, Dad, but I do trust my husband."

"Maybe you shouldn't."

"Do you mind telling me exactly what you're talking about? You've hinted at some subterfuge from the moment we started this conversation. If you know something unsavory about Drew, just tell me."

Her heart was knocking at jackhammer pace. *Please don't let there be anything, Lord.*

Her father slid open the top desk drawer and withdrew a large manila envelope.

"It hurts me, honey, to show you this." He pushed the envelope toward her. "But I have to. You're my only child and I'll do anything to protect you."

As soon as her fingers touched the paper, her stomach began to ache. A terrible foreboding kept her from taking the envelope.

"What is it?" Her words came out in a choked whisper.

"I had a private investigator check into Drew's background."

She shot up out of the chair. "You did what?"

"I only want what's best for you, Larissa. Sit down and read the report before you blast me. I'm not the one you should be angry with."

Feeling betrayed by her father's actions, she peeled back the flap on the envelope and slid out a thick file.

Drew's roguish face smiled up at her. She slammed the file down onto the desk. "I don't want to know."

Scared out of her mind, certain that her whole world was about to collapse, she wanted to run home to Drew.

Thomas circled the desk. "Hiding from the truth won't change it."

He was right, of course. Even if she never read the detective's report, she'd always wonder.

Hands shaking, she took up the file again and began to read. After a few pages, she looked up. Her father, love and concern in his eyes, stood waiting to offer moral support.

"There's nothing here that I don't already know about Drew."

"That's exactly the point."

"I don't know what you mean."

"Look closely at the dates. Drew Michaels, successful photographer, world traveler, and the man you married—" he put a hand on her shoulder "—doesn't exist."

Larissa didn't remember leaving the office building. She did recall reading the file over and over again. Her father was right. Drew suddenly appeared, like a phoenix from the ashes, in Oklahoma City at age eighteen. Before that, he didn't exist. Even the birth certificate was false, unrecorded in the state's vital records.

She pressed the gas pedal of her SUV, driving faster than was prudent. Her chest hurt from the welling sobs.

There had to be an explanation. But the official documents pounded at her. Drew had lied. He had falsified everything he was.

"Oh, Drew, what have you done? Why did you lie to me? Who are you?"

The tears broke then, blurring her vision. She swiped angrily at them. A husband who lied wasn't worth tears.

Her father was right. Only a man with something terrible to hide faked a completely new identity.

Who was Drew Michaels? A fortune hunter? A mass murderer? One of those men with wives strung all over the planet?

She sobbed harder. With all the traveling he did, that's exactly who he could be. She'd seen them on talk shows and news programs. Men who lived double lives.

Or someone worse. The possibilities were endless and frightening.

A traffic light loomed ahead, still green, so she gunned the motor. She had to get home. To confront Drew with this information. Maybe he could explain.

The light turned yellow.

Brakes squealed, and she yanked her head around to see a blue car bearing down on her.

Horns blared.

She screamed.

In the next instant, she cleared the light and the blue car sped past her, the driver's fist raised in anger.

Shaking from head to toe, she drove on, pressing faster and harder to get to Drew.

Her father had pleaded with her to go to her parents' house. He'd offered to call her mother. She laughed wildly. Her mother. Some help she'd be.

Maybe she should call Pastor Nelson. He'd know what to advise or at least pray with her until she was calm again.

But no. This was between her and Drew. She didn't want anyone else to know how stupid and gullible she'd been. She also didn't want to do anything that could hurt Drew. Whatever his reason for the changed identity, she loved him.

"Help me, Lord," she prayed through hot tears and an aching chest. "I don't know what to do."

She turned into the exclusive housing development and drove past the homes of Tulsa's most influential citizens. From the outside, each of them lived perfect lives, but she knew better. They all had problems, some worse than others. The outward trappings were just that—a facade, like her husband.

Who was he? What was he hiding?

As she turned into the driveway, Larissa tried to staunch the racking sobs. Facing Drew would be hard enough; she needed control.

Still, the tears flowed on.

Around the corner of the house, her husband ambled toward her, smiling, the limp less noticeable today. Coco trotted beside him, smiling, too.

Larissa's battered heart threatened to shatter. How could she still love him so much?

For the fraction of a second needed to grab a Kleenex, she took her eyes off the driveway.

As if her day couldn't get worse, she heard a thump and then a terrible scream.

"Coco!" Drew yelled and broke into a limping run.

The world tilted into the bizarre state of slow motion that occurs during an accident. Drew running. Coco screaming in pain. Larissa frozen in horror by the little dog writhing on the concrete.

By the time she fumbled out of the vehicle, Drew had scooped Coco into his hands and was yelling for her to get back inside.

Completely wrung out, she cried, "You drive."

As gently as possible, she took Coco and climbed into the passenger's seat. Drew roared into action.

She had cried all the way home, but now she sobbed and sobbed and sobbed, releasing the pain of Drew's betrayal along with the horror of running over her own dog.

"It's okay, baby," Drew kept saying. "You didn't see her. It's okay."

"She'll die. She'll die. I'll lose her, too." Tears rained down on the moaning, shivering little Yorkie.

"We're not losing her." He set his jaw in grim determination and slammed the accelerator to the floor.

The trip to the animal hospital took ten minutes. Though the detective's report lingered in the back of her mind, Larissa concentrated on her pet. In her out-of-control state, she'd been the one to injure Coco.

No matter what Drew had done or hadn't done, he stood beside her like a rock, arm firmly holding her together. Over and over, he murmured words of comfort and encouragement that only broke her heart more.

He loved her. She loved him. Why couldn't life be that simple?

The vet, after a sedative and x-rays, came into the waiting room. Her first words were the best news Larissa had heard all day.

"Coco will heal," the doctor said. "Her right foot is broken, her shoulder was dislocated and she has a number of bruises. I want to keep her overnight, but if everything goes as I expect, you can pick her up in the morning."

As soon as the verdict was rendered, Larissa fell into Drew's arms and sobbed some more.

"Hey, I told you she'd make it," he said gently, stroking her back and hair as if she were a child. The man had no clue that her tears were a confused mixture of everything that had happened today.

After the trauma of Coco's accident, Larissa had no strength left to ask Drew about the private investigator's report.

Whatever his secret, it would have to wait.

Two days later, Drew lay on the floor of their bedroom next to Coco's basket unaware that Larissa watched him from the hallway. He'd fried and crumbled bacon and was now patiently hand-feeding the little dog.

"A bum leg is no fun, huh, girl?" he murmured. Coco stared up at him with big, sad eyes. He gently bumped her lips with a piece of bacon. "Your favorite. Come on. Eat for Daddy."

The term tore at Larissa. *Daddy.* Foolish though it be, she wanted Drew to be the daddy of her children regardless of who he was or what he'd done.

Could his secret past be the reason he didn't want to have a baby?

She gripped the door facing, so wrung out with emotion she could hardly focus. She couldn't sleep, couldn't eat, and Drew thought Coco was the reason.

Every time she opened her mouth to ask him about the report, she lost her nerve. As she'd told her father from the beginning, she didn't want to know. She couldn't *bear* to know.

This was the Drew she knew and loved. The one who had slept on the floor next to her dog for the last two nights. The Drew who had told her over and over that the accident was not her fault. The Drew who kept trying to cheer her up with silly jokes, hugs, and even a bouquet of flowers.

She trusted him. As dumb as that sounded, she couldn't believe that *her* Drew had done anything terrible. There had to be a good reason why he kept his background a secret.

"Cody and Kelli want to know if Coco can have visitors," she said, trying to pretend that everything was normal.

He looked up and smiled. Her stomach did a somersault.

"What do you think?"

"They know to keep her calm and quiet."

"Then I say yes, maybe this afternoon after her nap."

Larissa rolled her eyes. "She naps all the time."

Drew dusted bacon crumbs from his fingers and sat up. He patted the carpet next to him, and she joined him.

"What have you been doing?"

She'd been on the phone with her father, making sure he didn't interfere again. If she was ever to know the truth, Drew would have to tell her himself.

"Talking to my dad."

"Campaign stuff?"

She nodded and scooted back against the wall. Drew came with her and they sat together watching their pet doze. When he leaned forward, the fish necklace swung out.

She touched his throat. "Tell me again when you got this necklace."

"A friend."

If she asked the right questions, perhaps the truth would come out on its own.

"You've told me that. But who was the friend?"

He gave her a curious look. "A teacher, when I was a kid."

"Can teachers do that?"

"I guess they can. Anyway, he did. He was a counselor. A Christian guy, real nice."

"Why did he give it to you?"

Drew got quiet. Had she struck a nerve?

"He gave them to lots of kids, not just me." He peered down at her, quizzical. "Why the twenty questions?"

"Just curious." She shrugged as if the answer didn't matter. "You've told me so little about your childhood. I don't know your parents' names or even where you went to school. You know those things about me."

She held her breath, hoping to glean some simple, sensible explanation for his empty past.

"That's because you're interesting and I'm not."

"That is so not true. You must have been an adorable little boy."

"Of course I was. Almost as adorable as I am now."

She bumped his arm. "Be serious."

"What else is there to know? I was a pain-in-the-neck kid with two great brothers. I lived in Oklahoma City. I had my first photography job at the big daily newspaper. A guy named Dwayne taught me everything about taking pictures. What else is there?"

You tell me, she wanted to say. Instead she asked, "Where did you go to school?"

"Would you believe me if I said Harvard?"

"Only if it's true."

He laughed. "It's not." He hooked an elbow around her neck and tugged. "Did I ever tell you

how much I like that little freckle right there?"
He kissed the spot beside her lip.

"Don't try to distract me." She pushed him
away. "Where did you go to school?"

"Oklahoma City," he said, frustrating her.
She wanted place names, people names.

"Which school?"

"Several of them." His face darkened. "We
moved a lot. I was such a rotten student I've
tried to forget my school days."

In an intentional avoidance maneuver Drew
twisted away to focus on Coco. The dog was
sound asleep.

Her questions were obviously making him
fidgety.

She placed a hand in the center of his tense
back. Softly, she asked, "Was your childhood
that bad, honey? Is that why you get this way
when I ask?"

Over one shoulder he gazed at her, expression bleak. In a harsh whisper, he said, "Yeah.
It was. Can we drop the subject, please?"

Whatever had happened to Drew had cut
deep and left scars. As much as she wanted to
know, Larissa backed off. Someday perhaps
he'd trust her enough to reveal his inner

torment. Even if he never did, she would love the Drew he was now. And pray with all her heart that the secret wouldn't someday destroy their marriage and shatter her heart.

Chapter Twelve

Coco's road to recovery was shorter than Drew's although the little dog played her injury to the hilt. Neither of her owners could refuse her anything, from hand-feeding to endless games with her squeaky toy.

"She's using your guilt against you," Drew said.

"And you're just a big pushover." Larissa lay on a patio lounger in the bright sunshine catching some rays. Coco, splinted foot aloft, lay on her back in Larissa's lap.

Since Coco's accident, Drew had felt different. Or perhaps the change had begun in Charleston. He wasn't sure. But he was strangely content these days, the constant pressure to be on the move lessened.

He still believed he wasn't good enough for Larissa, but for some unfathomable reason, he made her happy. He'd battled long and hard to help her see how worthless he was, but he'd lost. Somehow she'd turned the tables on him, and now he was scared of losing her.

The ironic notion made him laugh.

So, he'd come to a decision. If he could convince his lovely bride to raise dogs instead of children, maybe they had a chance. Maybe he could pretend to be the man she wanted. Maybe she would never have to know about his past. He'd do just about anything for her, so why not go on living the lie if that pleased his beautiful wife?

First, though, he'd make sure she wouldn't be stuck with a blind photographer who couldn't pay his own bills.

"I think I'm jealous," he said. "Coco's getting all the attention now."

Larissa pushed a pair of sunglasses onto her head and sat up, careful not to upset the dog.

"You're as spoiled as she is."

"I like it, too." He hunkered down beside the chair. "Not counting the stiff ankle, though, I'm close to one hundred percent. Well, maybe seventy-five."

In other words, he no longer felt as weak as a wet noodle.

"What about your vision? You've said nothing about it since Charleston."

"No more blackouts." Though the double vision came and went a lot. It stressed him. No use stressing her.

She stroked the side of his face with her fingertips. "I'm glad."

Basking in the glow of her love, he pressed a kiss to her palm. "But just in case, my agent and I have been doing some business on the phone."

"What do you mean, just in case?" She sat up and glared at him. Coco awakened and stretched. "You are not going to lose your sight, Drew. Too many people are praying."

He hoped prayer worked, but he wasn't counting on it.

"Hear me out. Shelby had an interesting proposition." His ankle started to throb, so he moved to the end of Larissa's lounger. "She thinks we should do a book, one of those coffee table things."

"That's a magnificent idea."

He thought so, too. Even if the lights went out for good, he had enough photographs on hand to sell individually or in books to make a living for a long time.

"A couple of publishers have expressed interest in a book of my kid shots. If that does well, we could do more." And then he'd know he could support his wife.

"Oh, it will. I just know it." She folded her long, elegant legs under her and leaned forward to grab his hand. "Your photos of children are stunning. Some of them move me to tears. Others make me smile. They're powerful, Drew. The public will love them."

He laughed, thrilled by her enthusiasm. "You're my best cheerleader."

"That's because I've seen the pictures. I don't think you realize how special they are. But when the public sees them, you may end up doing book tours and talk shows."

"That's what Shelby said, too." The whole idea of publicity made him nervous, though, so he planned to pass on that little perk. Someone out there might recognize him, then all his deception and planning would be for naught. Husband of a senator's daughter, famous photographer of children arrested for killing a bunch of kids.

Not good.

The dark cloud of doubt descended.

"I'll have to give the idea more thought."

"Go with it. It's a wonderful concept. And you wouldn't need to travel all the time."

"I've thought of that, too."

"Would you mind?"

He recognized the pinch of worry and knew his restless wandering had caused it. All during their marriage, Larissa had taken a backseat to his work. A woman like her, who deserved the world. The ugly truth of his neglect grieved him.

Slowly, he shook his head. "You know, as surprising as this may be, I wouldn't." He tickled the bottom of her foot. "Hanging out with you is kinda fun."

She wiggled her toes. "Told you."

"The city is doing a building demolition late this afternoon," he said. "I promised Ryan we'd go down after school and see what we can shoot."

"You've captivated that kid. The Radcliffs say he's even doing better in school."

"That's because I told him if his grades didn't improve, he couldn't use my darkroom."

"Ah, bribery."

"It works. Now what must I bribe you with to get a kiss before I leave?"

Her perfect mouth bowed in a smile. "Chocolate is good. Or roses."

He removed his shades and leaned in. The scent of coconut lotion filled his senses. "Sorry, all out. Anything else you want?"

A look flickered across her violet eyes, but she didn't answer. Instead, she grabbed his shirt collar and pulled him to her for a mind-numbing, blood-rushing kiss.

Drew was certain his eyes, blurry before, were now crossed.

When she released him, he leaned back, bemused. "Wow."

She took the dog from him. "Too bad you have to run off."

"No kidding," he said and started toward the door. "Why did I tell Ryan I would pick him up from school?"

His wife's delicious giggle followed him into the house.

Larissa stroked Coco's silky fur, her heart singing as Drew left. Every day she fell more in love with him. Whoever Drew Michaels had been before, he was a good man now. Let the past remain buried.

When he'd jokingly asked what she wanted, she'd almost said a baby, but that particular subject hadn't been broached since Charleston.

Drew had promised to think about it and she wanted to give him plenty of time.

Taking her lotion and her dog, she went into the house.

Why was she lying to herself? She didn't mention a baby because she was afraid of his reaction. Things had been going so smoothly. Drew was attending church and asking very astute questions, most of which she couldn't answer. Fortunately, Mark and Drew had become friendly enough to spend a little time together. According to her husband, Mark was pretty smart about the Bible.

She could only keep praying that the little fish around Drew's neck would soon come to have real meaning.

After a quick shower, she grabbed a bottle of water from the fridge and turned on the television. The local news had interviewed her dad about a government scam he'd uncovered and the piece had gained national attention. According to his office, the interview would air today. She shoved a tape into the recorder. As part of her father's campaign team, she routinely gathered tidbits and sound bites for his ads.

As her dad's familiar baritone filled the living room, pride swelled in Larissa's chest. Thomas

Stone was the best congressman in the state, even if she did say so. Though unhappy about the investigation, she knew her father had only been trying to protect her.

She settled back against the couch cushions, letting her wet hair dry naturally while the news ran.

Later, she and Drew had tickets for a touring Broadway play at the Performing Arts Theater, but she had plenty of time to get ready.

The sun had made her lazy. Curling her feet onto the sofa, she stretched out and thought about what she'd wear tonight. The news played on but she paid it no mind.

Last week, she'd purchased a pair of strappy heels that would look great with a short cocktail dress. Maybe the blue one Drew liked so much.

Suddenly, an image on the television caught her attention. Two male hands each holding a small, pewter key chain in the shape of a Jesus fish.

"Separated as boys, reunited as men," the narrator's voice intoned. "Connected by one brother's memory and the Christian symbol that each carried in his pocket. Coincidence? Or divine intervention?"

The poignantly beautiful shot faded to black.

A tingle went down Larissa's spine. She sat straight up, lazy no more.

Drew wore an ichthus exactly like that.

She tried to blow off the strange sensation. Lots of people had Jesus fish these days.

The eerie feeling wouldn't go away.

To satisfy her curiosity, Larissa rewound the tape to the beginning of the piece, the section she'd missed.

The reporter started the story, introducing the two brothers, one a cop in Oklahoma City, the other a street minister in New Orleans.

Larissa listened with rapt attention. Something about the tall, dark brother was familiar. His sculpted cheekbones, square jaw and darkly intense eyes reminded her so much of Drew. It was weird. Too weird.

With expert skill, the narrator wove a heartbreaking story of three brothers, separated by foster care as children.

She frowned. Three brothers? But there were only two in the story.

"Collin Grace would not give up the search," the reporter said. "For more than twenty years he searched for his brothers, only to discover that Drew had died in a fire at age fifteen."

Collin and Drew!

Blood rushed through her ears with such force, she could hardly hear the program. But she tried not to jump to conclusions. There were lots of men in the world named Collin and Drew.

"Ian Carpenter, the youngest of the three brothers had been adopted by a Louisiana family."

Now she was shaking all over. Drew had told her his brothers' names. Ian and Collin.

But that made no sense. According to her husband, his brothers had died in a fire. According to this news report, Drew had died in a fire. They couldn't be the same set of brothers. Could they?

As the news story drew to a close, Larissa once more glimpsed the image of the men's hands, each bearing the fish symbol. A symbol that Drew also carried.

She hit Rewind again, playing the tape over and over until her heart hammered so hard she wondered if she might pass out.

All three of the names were the same. The fish symbol, given to each boy by a school counselor, was the same. And even though the fire story was convoluted, it was still part of the story. Something was going on here. Could the missing brother, the one purported to have died in a fire, be her husband? Could something about this separation be the cause of Drew's secretiveness?

Trembling all over, but more excited than she'd been in ages, Larissa grabbed the telephone. As a congressman's daughter, she had a certain amount of clout. Someone at CNN could put her in contact with the original reporter of that story.

Within ten minutes she had the name of Gretchen Barker, a journalist with Channel Eleven news in New Orleans. She called the station only to discover that Ms. Barker was not working that day. After breathlessly explaining the situation, she was relieved to hear that the producer would give the reporter a message and ask her to contact Larissa ASAP.

She hung up the phone, nervous as a cat on diet pills. If the reporter called back while Drew was here, what would she do? She couldn't lie to him, but if this was true and he was the missing brother, she wasn't sure how he would handle the news. After all, he'd hidden the truth for years. There must be a reason.

Coco's fluffy head moved back and forth as Larissa paced from one side of the room to the other.

"Your daddy has brothers," she said, chewing

on the side of her nail. "He needs them. They need him."

The memory of Collin Grace's face, so sorrowful for the lost brother and so overjoyed with the reunion, was imprinted on her mind. If Drew was his brother, the man deserved to know he was alive.

She paced to the window and looked out, praying that Drew wouldn't return before Gretchen Barker called.

Throat dry with nerves, she gulped down the rest of her water.

Still no call. She played the tape again.

Halfway through, the phone chirped.

Punching Pause, she vaulted from the chair and ripped the receiver from the hook. "Hello."

A woman's smooth, professional voice said, "This is Gretchen Barker with Channel Eleven News in New Orleans. May I speak with Larissa Michaels?"

"This is she."

"I understand you may have some information about the reunion story I did on two brothers."

"Ms. Barker, this may sound crazy, but I think the third brother, Drew, may still be alive."

She quickly apprised Gretchen of the evidence, delighted when the reporter concurred.

"Larissa," she said. "I hope you don't mind if I call you that. You see, we may be relatives soon. I'm engaged to Ian Carpenter."

"Oh, my goodness." Larissa's head swam with emotion and excitement. "This is amazing."

"I think you may be on to something. At least I hope you are. But we can't be sure until you to talk to Collin. He remembers more about the boys' childhood than anyone, which isn't pretty, by the way, so prepare yourself. I told him about your call to the station. He said if there was even the most remote chance that you had information on Drew he wants to talk to you. I'm a skeptical reporter, but from what you've told me, I think there's more than a remote chance."

Larissa's hand trembled as she grabbed for a pencil. "Do you have his number?"

A thousand questions raced through Larissa's mind, but she saved them for Collin. If he and Drew were brothers, he would know.

"Not only do I have his number, I have the man himself. He's in the next room."

"Oh. Oh, my goodness. I can't believe this is happening." Adrenaline rushed to her head. She took a deep breath to clear the powerful jumble of nerves.

"I can't either, but it's wonderful. Can you

hold on or would you like for him to call you back privately?"

"Actually, I could use a minute to gather my thoughts. If you'll give me his number, I'll call him right back."

"Sure. He'll probably feel the same way." Gretchen rattled off an area code right there in Oklahoma and then added her own cell number.

Somehow, Larissa thanked Gretchen properly and rang off. Her hands shook.

After checking the front window to be sure Drew had not returned, she drew in a deep, shaky breath and punched in Collin's number, throat so full of emotion she wasn't sure she could even speak.

He answered on the first ring. "Grace."

Unsure of how to begin, she blurted, "This is Larissa Michaels. I think I'm married to your brother."

A sharp inhale and then, "Tell me why you think so."

Collin's voice was tense and steel-edged. He was trying hard to be an unemotional cop. He was failing. The hope zinging through the wires ripped at Larissa. This mattered even more to him than it did to her.

"His name is Drew, and he's told me he had

two brothers, Ian and Collin, in Oklahoma City, but he says they died in a fire along with the rest of his family."

"The names fit but not the fire."

"He wears a Jesus fish on a necklace that looks exactly like yours and Ian's. He never takes it off and acts funny whenever I ask about it."

"Funny? In what way?"

"Secretive. Dark. Almost depressed. He's shared very little with me about his past."

"Why?"

"I was hoping you could help me clear up the mystery."

"I'm a police officer who deals in facts and evidence. Any of this could be coincidence, but…" His voice trailed off, lost in thought.

Larissa picked up on his longing. "But you want your brother to be alive."

He drew a ragged breath. "Yeah. Tell me everything he's ever mentioned. Any little detail."

She did, including the story of the hiding place in the woods and carrying Ian on his back. It sounded like such a small amount.

"I'm embarrassed to know so little about the man I've been married to for more than three years."

"It's enough." Collin's words were tight with

excitement. "He's my brother. That's Drew. Everything fits except the fire."

Larissa's heart lurched. "But why has he lied about you? Why has he kept his childhood a secret?"

"Shame. Pride. I don't know."

"He has nothing to be ashamed of." But she knew it was exactly the kind of thing Drew would do. He was a proud man.

"What about the fire? Why would he lie about that?"

"I don't know. There *was* a fire and several people died, but the records list Drew as one of the dead."

"I can't figure out what could have happened, can you? According to a private investigator, Drew Michaels suddenly began to exist at the age of eighteen. There's no record of him before that."

"You had him investigated?" Ice dripped from the words, accusing her.

"No. My father did. And Drew has no idea, so please keep this between us."

Silence hummed over the line. She'd upset him.

"Mr. Grace, please. I love my husband. I mean him no harm, ever. I only want to help him. Why else would I be calling you?"

Finally, he relented. She could almost hear

his cop brain working as he put together all the evidence.

"What date did the P.I. first encounter a record of your husband's existence?"

She named the year. "Why?"

"You've just sealed the case. That's the same year my brother supposedly died in a fire."

"But it brings me right back to the same question. Why all the secrecy?"

"Drew is the only one who can explain what happened, but in my line of work I've encountered stranger occurrences. Sometimes people want a change, want to start over. Considering the kind of childhood we led, it would be understandable."

"Would I be out of line to ask about your childhood?"

After a moment of hesitation, he said, "I've hidden my background all my life, too. Not in the way Drew apparently has, but it's not something I like to talk about. I'd rather Drew told you."

"So would I, but he hasn't."

"Just suffice it to say, we lived a hard life. Our mother was a crack addict who left us for days at a time. When she was home, she wasn't always nice. Drew knows what it is to be hungry and scared and helpless. Getting separated from each other was the worst thing that ever happened to us. To me anyway."

"Oh, Collin." Pain tore a hole in her heart. "I'm so sorry. So, so sorry." The pieces of her husband's puzzle began to fall into place. "I understand now why he didn't tell me."

And why he was so reluctant to have a baby. He must be terrified of repeating the ugly cycle. *Oh, my precious husband.* The love inside her tripled. What an admirable, resilient man she'd married.

"I don't know how to thank you," Collin said. "I searched for such a long time and now to find both my brothers in the space of a few months. God is awesome."

"Yes, He is." A smile bloomed. "I take it you're a Christian, too."

"A new one, thanks to my fiancée and her family. I never put much stock in God before but now I know the Bible verse on this key chain is true." He jiggled something against the receiver. "In all these years God has never forsaken us. We've had rough times, but God has always worked things for our good."

"Now I realize God used Drew's accident as a way to reunite the three of you." She didn't add that the accident had also given her and

Drew time to mend their marital problems. After all, Collin was a stranger.

"What accident? Is my brother okay?"

She briefly filled him in on Drew's line of work, the explosion, and his recovery.

When she finished, Collin said, "I'm only a couple of hours away. How about if I drive up there tonight? Or tomorrow, if that's better?"

Larissa felt his eagerness over the phone, but she was not ready for this. Drew had no idea what she'd done.

She put a hand to her forehead. "I'm not sure that's a good idea. I haven't had time to absorb all this, much less break it to Drew. I only saw the news clip about a half hour ago."

"Lady, I've been waiting for more than twenty years. I want to see my brother."

"I understand that, but I need time to gauge how he feels, what he wants. He's hidden his past for a reason. He may need some time."

"I want to talk to him. To see him. He's my brother."

"Soon. I promise."

Collin's yearning was getting to her in a hurry. More rattled now than ever, she said a quick goodbye and hung up.

Both thrilled and terrified, she sat on the sofa,

telephone receiver clasped to her chest and prayed. All the while, her mind raced.

How was Drew going to react to this news? Had he ever tried to find his lost siblings? Did he even want to? Worse yet, what if Collin told him about the private investigator? Without a doubt, Drew would not react well to that little piece of information.

She pinched her lips together, thinking.

Tonight was the play, but perhaps they should cancel. She was too overwrought at the moment to enjoy an evening out. She needed time alone with her husband. A revelation of this proportion required exactly the right time and the right mood.

But she couldn't cancel. She'd looked forward to this play for months and Drew knew it. He'd ordered the tickets as a sweet surprise for her. If she canceled now, he would know something was amiss. And his feelings would be hurt.

"Lord, please help. I don't know what to do. I fear I've opened a can of worms that will only make matters worse. If Drew wanted me to know, he would have told me."

The fact that he hadn't trusted her enough sliced deeply.

How in the world would she ever find a way

to tell him that she knew about his secret past? The past he'd tried so hard to leave behind?

Would he be angry? Would he hate her for prying?

A thousand thoughts swirled in her head, fast and confusing.

With an anxious groan, she went to the bedroom to fix her hair for the play.

Chapter Thirteen

"What's wrong, sweetheart?"

Drew watched his wife remove a pair of long, glittering earrings and drop them on the dresser. She'd been super quiet tonight, her thoughts a thousand miles away. "You haven't been yourself. Didn't you like the play?"

"I have a headache."

"Why didn't you say something earlier?" The artsy play scene wasn't all that important. He would have brought her home.

She shrugged, saying nothing, as distracted now as she had been all evening.

"Are you sure that's all?"

He stood behind her, watching her beautiful face in the mirror. Her gaze rose to meet his, then quickly shifted away. A tiny furrow pinched her eyebrows together.

Drew couldn't help wonder if he'd done something to upset her.

He placed his hands on her bare shoulders and began to massage, breathing in the sweet, clean smell of her hair.

"Tension?"

She nodded, letting her head tilt from side to side. After a minute, she reached back and patted his hands. "I think I'll take some aspirin and go to bed."

A faint twinge of disappointment hit him. Usually she loved his massages. He dropped his hands and watched her head for the bathroom to change.

The play was one she'd anticipated for months, but she'd barely said a word about it.

Something more than a headache was bothering his wife. And it worried him for more reasons than one.

Tossing his jacket onto the back of a chair, he went to check on Coco. When he returned with the dog and her basket, Larissa was already in bed, her back turned. Only the lamp on his side burned.

As quietly as possible, he prepared for bed, then snapped off the light.

Larissa didn't stir.

After a few seconds, he whispered, "I love you."

There was no answer. She must have been asleep already.

He lay in the darkness wondering. Was it the baby thing again? One of the couples they'd met for coffee during the intermission had announced a baby on the way. Larissa had not been the same since.

No, there was something else. He could feel it. She was keeping something from him. Tomorrow, after she was rested and the headache cured, he would ask.

Drew awakened to the sound of Coco's insistent whine. Scrubbing both hands over his sleepy face, he sat up. Daylight flooded the room.

"What time is it?" He twisted around to ask Larissa.

Her side of the bed was empty.

"Uh-oh. We've overslept again, Coco. Mommy's already up." He scratched at his chest and looked around. "Wonder why she didn't take you out?"

He and the dog limped through the house. The ankle was stiff in the morning, but limbered up as the day progressed.

He sniffed the air. Coffee was on. Thank goodness. But no sign of Larissa.

"Maybe she took a swim."

Outside, he placed Coco on the ground to do her business and went toward the pool house.

Larissa wasn't there either.

For a minute, he stood in the yard, thinking.

Had she mentioned going anywhere this morning?

With Coco in tow, he returned to the kitchen for much needed coffee. There he found a note stuck to the coffeepot.

"Mother's decorator is coming this morning. She needs my input. Back by noon."

"Should have guessed," he groused.

He had work to do in the darkroom anyway, though Larissa's company down there was way better than the teenage Ryan's. But Ryan wasn't coming either. He had school.

"Just me and you, girl," he said. Coco's response was a baleful stare that made him chuckle.

The morning flew by. He developed photos,

talked to his agent, sorted kid pictures that he thought might work in this book idea of hers.

That whole thing freaked him out, but it was good, too. With books in the works, he'd have an income regardless of what happened with the vision.

And the books would make Larissa happier, too. He could stay home more. He'd never been in one spot very long, and wasn't sure how he would feel in the long run. But being here with Larissa all this time had settled him in a way he hadn't thought possible. He loved waking up to her. Truth be told, he didn't trust his eyes enough to travel much right now.

At noon, he went upstairs to grab a bite. He was creating the world's fattest sandwich when the phone rang. Expecting Larissa, he grabbed for it.

"Hello."

An unfamiliar masculine voice said, "Is this Drew?"

Cradling the phone between shoulder and ear, he smeared mayo on a slice of bread. "In the flesh. Who am I talking to?"

There was an eerie pause.

Telemarketer, Drew thought and started to hang up.

"Drew." The man sounded choked. "This is Collin."

The knife in Drew's hand clattered against the jar. "Collin?" He could barely whisper. "Collin who?"

But he knew. Even after all this time, he knew. There were thousands of men named Collin but this was the one.

"Your brother. I've found Ian, too. He's on his way here now."

All the air whooshed out of Drew's lungs. He stumbled to a bar stool and collapsed. "My brother. Where? How? Oh, man. Is it really you?"

A soft chuckle reassured him. "Yeah, it's me, you little twerp. Where have you been hiding?"

It was his big brother all right. And Drew didn't know how to act. "It's been twenty years."

"More than that. I'm sorry to catch you by surprise like this. I was actually calling to speak to Larissa, but when I heard your voice, I couldn't wait any longer."

Elbow on the breakfast bar, Drew leaned his head on one palm. His mind swam, as jumbled as his emotions. "Why would you want to talk to my wife?"

Another long pause. "She didn't tell you."

"Tell me what?"

"That she and I talked yesterday. Between the two of us we figured out the truth, that you're my long missing, presumed dead brother."

"Larissa knows?" All of a sudden, her strange behavior last night came into focus. She *knew*.

That's why she hadn't welcomed his massage. That's why she'd hardly talked to him at the play. That's why she'd turned her back and pretended to be asleep when he whispered his love.

The sense of loss engulfed him. In finding his brothers, he was losing his wife. This time the rift would be too big to mend.

He could never repair the damage he'd done by marrying her under false pretenses. And now she knew. At least part of it. Now, it was only a matter of time until she discovered the rest.

"As I said, Ian is on his way here now," Collin was saying. "We want to come to Tulsa and meet you. We've got a lot of catching up to do."

Drew sat bolt upright. "No. Not here. I mean, where are you? I'll come there."

"Works for me. I'm in Oklahoma City."

Oklahoma City. All this time his brother was less than two hours away. Reeling from the information, he couldn't think straight. One thing kept coming back to him. Larissa knew. She knew he was nothing. She knew he was a fraud and a fake.

Everything in him screamed denial. He'd tried so hard to keep the ugliness away, only to have it return in the form of a brother he loved.

How did he reconcile the two?

The fact was, he couldn't.

The world he'd created was coming to an end. Larissa knew about him, and their life together was over. Oh, she'd deny that his background made a difference, but her actions last night told the tale. She'd never accept his life of lies.

With a mix of joy and sadness, he made arrangements to meet his brothers.

Slowly, he replaced the receiver and sat staring at it. His sandwich waited on the counter, but his appetite was gone. Like a man in a trance, he put away the food and went to pack his clothes.

His instincts had been right after all. He never should have come back here.

Might as well make the break and save the humiliation of being ordered to get out.

As he pulled jeans and boots from the closet, Coco managed to leave her basket and toddle into the bedroom, tags jingling. She cocked her head at him as if to say, "Are you leaving again?"

"Daddy's gotta go, girl." The word daddy choked him.

Larissa wanted kids. Once he was out of her life, she could find someone else, a man who wasn't afraid to give her the babies she wanted so badly.

He sat down on the side of the bed, his whole being screaming against the decision. Larissa with someone else? He'd thought he had that all settled in his head months ago. He'd been wrong. The notion tore him apart.

Back to square one. She deserved far better than a throwaway kid with bad genes and a worse track record. Now that his identity had been revealed, the rest of the story would soon come out.

He wouldn't saddle her with a convict.

He glanced at the clock—already past noon and Larissa's promised return time. Not that he was surprised. A trip to her demanding mother's was never as short or as simple as she planned.

And then again, maybe she was avoiding him now that she knew.

In too short a time, he was packed. He traveled light. Mostly his camera equipment and a few clothes. When the smoke cleared, he'd send word for her to give his other things to Goodwill.

For now, he'd head to the city for a few days, get reacquainted with his brothers. By then he'd have a job. As scared as he was to travel, he was more afraid to stay. Afraid to face Larissa. Afraid that a restless wanderer couldn't survive in an eight-by-ten cell.

He wasn't much else, but he was a survivor.

Backpack slung over one shoulder, he picked up his duffel bag and headed to the kitchen. He couldn't just walk out without at least scribbling a note. Larissa would worry. No matter what she thought of him, his sweet wife would still worry.

His lips twisted bitterly. What did a man write at a time like this?

He started and stopped several times, ending up with wads of paper, before scratching out a quick note.

"That'll have to do." He stuck the note on her pillow then reshouldered his bag.

Coco tried to follow him to the door. He picked her up, pressed the warm, soft little body to his face. "Take care of her, girl."

As he walked out into the clear spring afternoon, closing the door of the only home he'd ever known, the wound in Drew's soul reopened and started to bleed.

He checked into a small hotel off Interstate 40 before driving to meet his brothers. Sick to his stomach with emotion, he couldn't eat, so he stopped at a convenience store for antacids and a bottle of water.

Finding Collin and Drew had always been in the back of his mind, but he'd wanted to do it on his time and in his way. Not like this. Not when opening the door to the past cost him so dearly.

Directions to Collin's farm on the seat beside him, he made the trip west of the city where the houses grew farther apart and dirt roads took the place of pavement. The countryside was in bloom, a gorgeous feast for a photographer's eyes.

He could imagine Collin out here in the country.

The phone call had been such a shock he'd failed to learn much about his brothers' lives. He hoped they had both been happy.

When he spotted the half-finished house surrounded by animal pens and a big new barn, he knew this had to be Collin's place.

A grin broke over his face.

His big brother hadn't changed. He'd always provide for an animal first and himself second.

As soon as the thought came, he sobered. Collin had provided for Ian and him first, as well. He'd been the best big brother any boy could ever have, and Drew was truly sorry they'd spent all these years apart.

He pulled next to a late-model SUV and killed the engine. Palms clammy against the steering wheel, he licked dry lips. He was literally scared spitless.

What did he say to two brothers who were strangers? Would they be angry that he'd never searched for them? Would he have the nerve and the faith in their brothers' bond to tell them the reason?

The front door opened. A shaggy little dog with three legs bounded from the house, pink tongue bobbing.

"Might as well get out, Michaels," he muttered, and then shook his head. What would Collin and Ian say to the name change?

Behind the small, delighted dog, a tall, dark man came into view. A man with an uncanny resemblance to himself.

Drew's heart lurched. *Collin.*

Every cell in his body cried out. This was his brother. His flesh and blood. So different, but still the same.

He pushed the car door open and managed to move forward, though he was wobbly enough to collapse.

"You grew up," he said.

"Makes two of us." Collin crossed the space between them and the two men stood taking each other's measure. "After Larissa told me about the explosion, I expected the worst. You look good, little brother. Real good."

They clasped firm handshakes, then clapped each other on the back, each uncertain how to behave but hungry to reclaim the lost years. To Drew's way of thinking, his brothers were now all he would have.

"Come on in. Ian's on the phone with his lady." Collin shot him a sideways grin. "The reporter in New Orleans who did the story."

Drew blinked, confused. "What story?"

"The news story Larissa saw. The one on Ian and me. None of us ever dreamed it would have this impact. But God knew what He was up to."

"I didn't know." When Collin turned to look at him, he clarified. "About the story. I didn't see it."

"Didn't you talk to Larissa before driving down here?"

Drew shook his head, not ready to go there.

"Well, come on in. We'll fill you in on everything." He held the storm door open. "It may take all night."

"Fine with me." The only place he had to go was a hotel room.

The three-legged dog whined and pushed against Collin's legs.

"This little annoyance is Happy," Collin said affectionately, bending to stroke the shaggy little animal.

Remembering Coco's sad eyes, Drew added a pat to the friendly head and stepped inside to meet his baby brother.

Ian came from the kitchen carrying a plate filled with pastries and three glasses of milk. He quickly plunked them onto a makeshift coffee table and grabbed Drew's hand.

"Man, it's good to see you," he said.

His open, friendly face was wreathed in smiles, and even as an adult he reminded Drew of a puppy. A good-looking puppy with gentle blue eyes and an aura of peace. Drew liked him all over again.

For the next two hours the three brothers renewed a long dormant relationship while they munched goodies from the Carano Bakery. The Caranos, he discovered, would soon be Collin's in-laws.

As they reminisced about crazy antics and good times, Drew was amazed at how good he felt to let the memories out again. For so long, he'd kept his brothers locked away in the back of his mind, afraid to go there.

He learned that Ian had been adopted into a happy home and now ran a mission for runaways in New Orleans. Collin, like him, grew up in the system, and now was not only an Oklahoma City police officer but also ran a rehab ranch for wounded and abandoned animals.

The avocation fit. It was the vocation that struck Drew as funny. It also terrified him.

"I still can't believe you're a cop." Drew shook his head at Collin. "After all the food we stole out of stores and gardens, I figured you'd be on the other side of the law." *Like me.*

Collin chuckled. "God has a sense of humor. That's for certain."

"And you, a preacher," he said to Ian. "I can see that. You were always the good one."

They all three chuckled. Collin said, "You were the one we figured would end up in jail. For years, I kept expecting to arrest you at any time."

The joke would have been funny if it wasn't so close to the truth. He couldn't even think of a clever comeback.

He stuffed his mouth with a cherry Danish, chewing thoughtfully. His brother was a cop. In all his searching for Drew and Ian, had Collin never looked into the records of the fire? Did he not know of Drew's crime? And if he did, would he feel duty bound to turn in his own brother?

A shiver of dread snaked up Drew's spine. His past was rapidly closing in on him. He definitely needed to make a quick exit out of the country.

The notion hurt like sticking his hand to a hot stove. This time, he didn't want to go. But he had to.

"So," he said, eager to change the subject before he broke down like a fool and confessed everything. "Tell me about these ladies you're engaged to."

Blue eyes twinkling, Ian rubbed his hands together with an eager excitement that was so like the little boy Drew remembered.

"I'm engaged to Gretchen, the most incredible, hardheaded, smart and sassy woman in New Orleans." While his brothers laughed at the description, he added, "She's the reporter who nagged us into doing that reunion story."

"I still haven't seen it," Drew admitted. That tiny segment had changed his life and he wanted to watch it for more reasons than one. He hoped the story didn't include anything that could lead Larissa to his worst nightmare. She didn't deserve the humiliation of knowing she'd loved a murderer. "Do you have the tape?"

"Are you kidding?" Ian asked. "Gretchen is so proud of that piece. She stuck three copies in my suitcase. I'll give you one to take home."

Home. Wherever that was.

But he only said, "That would be great. I appreciate it." He looked at Collin. "What about you? You engaged to a reporter, too?"

"Worse." Collin aimed a chocolate éclair at him, one eyebrow quirked exactly the way Drew recalled. The memory was sweet and unexpected. "Prepare yourself. This is gonna hurt. My lady, Mia, is a social worker."

Drew nearly choked on his Danish. When he'd managed to swallow the chunk, he said, "You have to be joking."

As kids, they had, all three, feared and despised social workers, seeing them as an enemy who would separate them. In the end, that's exactly what had happened.

"Nope. No joke at all. She's the best thing, after the Lord, that ever happened to me. Mia Carano. Kind, generous, beautiful, even if she is a social worker. I'm crazy about her." He chomped down onto the éclair. Mouth full, he muttered, "Terrific cook, too."

"Can't argue with that." Drew gulped a swig of milk and then helped himself to another sweet roll. "I'd like to meet them both."

And he meant it, too. Before he hit the road again, he wanted to know more about his brothers' lives, including the women who'd captured their hearts.

"Hey, we can arrange a meeting anytime," Collin said. "All you have to say is 'get-together,' and Mia and her big Italian family will whip into action, rustle up more food than anyone can eat, and invite us all to a three-day celebration."

The glow in Collin's dark eyes said he loved every minute of it, just as he loved his fiancée. Drew was glad. Truly. Collin deserved someone special to love him. Even if Mia Carano *was* a social worker, Drew liked her already.

"I see a big family reunion in our very near future," Ian said. "Gretchen is already talking about it. And she wants to report *that* story, too."

Collin groaned. "I figured as much."

"Hey, she's responsible for getting us three back together. Giving her another warm and fuzzy story is the least we can do."

"Just joking," Collin said. "I thank God for your nosey reporter fiancée. Without her, we'd never have found Drew."

They thanked God to have found him? The idea was humbling to say the least, and he hoped neither lived to regret the enthusiasm.

He was amazed that both of his brothers had somehow ended up as Christians. They sure hadn't learned about Jesus as kids. But now here they were talking about God the way Larissa did. Funny how that didn't make him uncomfortable. In fact, he wanted to know more.

For Larissa being a Christian was easy. She was already good. But how did men loaded down with their ugly baggage reconcile with a holy God?

"We're anxious to meet your wife, too," Ian said, bringing Drew back to the conversation.

The icing on his donut turned bitter. He gazed down at the maple glaze, the ache in his gut starting up again. "That's not going to be possible, guys. Sorry."

Collin narrowed his eyes, cop instinct flashing from him like a neon sign. "Why not?"

Drew sat there for a long moment, unsure of what to say. Should he blow off the question or tell the truth? Well, as much of the truth as he could. Collin was his big brother, but he was still a cop. Besides, Drew had no intention of laying something as heavy as the fire on his newly-found siblings. The situation with Larissa was heavy enough.

Heavy enough to break him in two.

Today had been a mixture of joy and grief. Right now, the grief was back.

Careful to keep the worst to himself, he admitted he was divorcing Larissa.

"I'm not even who I claimed to be. I'm nobody, married to a blue blood."

"What difference does that make?" Collin growled, his face intense.

Drew tossed the donut onto a napkin. "Don't you get it, Collin? I lied. I never told her who I really am. Even my name is false. She thought she married some hotshot photographer."

"She did."

He made a disparaging noise. "You of all people know better than that."

"You're not the same wild kid, Drew. That's obvious." Ian leaned forward, his earnest expression one of a both a minister and brother. "You've made a decent life for yourself. Don't blow it now just because Larissa found out about your sorry childhood."

"It's not just the lies I've told. She wants kids. A family. She wants me to settle down, stay home more."

"Pretty normal stuff for a married couple to want."

"She wants it. I don't." But as soon as he spoke, he knew the words were no longer true.

"Last night, she made it pretty clear that I was history. I didn't know why then. Now I do. Finding out that I have an ugly past must have been a big blow. Her father's a congressman. Skeletons in the closet are not acceptable."

Pinching his bottom lip, Ian leaned forward, elbows on his thighs. "Maybe. But did you ever think she might be struggling with how to tell you that your long-lost brother had called? You kept it secret. She had to wonder why. She had to wonder if you would be upset."

He hadn't considered that perspective.

His face must have said so, because Collin pressed the advantage. "She *was* worried about how you would take the news."

"Nice try, guys, but I don't think so. I'm a fake, a fraud. Larissa doesn't even carry my real name."

"Changing your name is no sin," Ian said. "I did it."

Drew made a disparaging noise. "You were adopted. No choice there. I took my name from a British rock star."

Collin laughed. Here Drew was bleeding all

over the place and his brother laughed at him. Some things didn't change.

No, not true. Some things did change. As a kid, he would have jumped up and punched Collin in the nose. Today, he saw the humor, too.

"I've made a mess of things. She's better off without me." He shook his head. "There are other problems."

"What kind of problems? If you need money…"

Ian's offer didn't surprise him at all, but he waved him off. "Money's not the issue. At least not at this point. But there are other reasons. Several of them. Too many and too serious to overcome."

Regardless of shared blood, these men were virtual strangers. He couldn't tell them about the crime and he wasn't ready to talk about his eyesight. He shifted gears. "Suffice it to say, I'm not good enough for her. I'm getting out of her life so she can be happy."

Ian's quiet eyes studied him. "Have you talked to Larissa about this?"

"Don't need to."

"Women always need to talk." One side of Collin's mouth jerked up in self-mockery. "I found *that* out the hard way."

"Maybe I'll call her later," Drew said. He wouldn't. No point in prolonging the inevitable.

Ian got up and crossed the narrow space between the couch and chair. His movements were quiet and carried with them a gentle assurance.

"Drew," he said, going down on one knee. "I remember the time we were walking on hot pavement. I was barefoot and my feet were burning, so you carried me on your back." Voice dropping to a hush, he touched Drew's shoulder. "But you didn't have any shoes either."

Drew swallowed hard, uncomfortable with his brother's emotion. What did a childhood memory have to do with his shattered life?

Ian squeezed Drew's shoulder. "You're my brother. I love ya, man. Always have. Always will. I think I have a right to pry into your personal business. So, don't be offended, but here goes."

"We've been prying into each others' business all evening," Drew answered. Not that he'd told them everything, but these two knew more about him than anyone else on the planet.

"Yeah, well this is real personal. Collin and I believe God brought us all back together. We give him the glory and praise for that."

"He was pretty slow about it."

"God's timing never suits me either, but the point is He does what He's promised." Ian took out his key chain and turned the silver fish on its back. He rubbed his finger across the words emblazoned on all their hearts. "A long time ago, He promised never to leave or forsake three terrified little boys. He kept that promise. Now we've come full circle, back together again."

"I'm not sure what this has to do with Larissa."

"Everything. Collin and I both had to deal with some issues from our childhood. Hurts, rejections, abandonment. God healed those."

Ian glanced at Collin who nodded his agreement.

"He'll heal yours, too, Drew. We were wounded kids. All of us. Wounded kids become wounded adults unless they get help. The best helper you'll ever find is Jesus Christ."

Drew had to agree with one thing. He was one messed up dude.

"I want to pray with you, bro. Can we do that?"

Drew's eyes flashed to Collin. His big brother rose from the chair to join Ian on the hardwood floor.

The sight of two grown men, both of them

about as manly as a man could be, on their knees, did something funny to Drew's insides.

It made him envious. They were so at peace. So certain they'd found the answers.

He wanted what his brothers and his wife had found.

"I'm not sure I know how," he admitted. "I mean, I've tried to pray. Larissa's a Christian, goes to church and all that stuff, but I don't know how to be one."

"Do you want to?" Ian's kind face was radiant. He must be a humdinger of a preacher. "Knowing Jesus is the easiest thing in the world."

"Tell me what to do and I'll do it."

"Just believe, brother. Just believe." And then Ian led him in a simple prayer, asking Jesus to come into his heart, to forgive his sins, to help him live a changed life.

As the words fell from his trembling lips, an incredible joy burst inside his soul. Light brighter than the sunrise filled his being.

When the prayer ended, he looked up. The room was the same. His brothers were the same. Except for the holy joy on their faces.

But he was different.

"Larissa talked about the light. I didn't know what she meant," he said in awe.

"The entire book of John talks about it, too. Jesus is the light. When you ask Him into your life, His light fills you. Five minutes ago, you were a child of darkness. Now you have come into God's marvelous light. You are heir to everything in God's kingdom, all the promises, including the right to ask Him to restore your marriage."

As reality tumbled back with a vengeance, Drew swallowed hard. Even though he was different on the inside, his exterior problems hadn't disappeared. "Marriage to me isn't the best thing for Larissa."

"You should let God decide that."

"Being a Christian doesn't change the mistakes I've made."

"No, but God has forgiven you. Maybe you should forgive yourself."

He wasn't sure if he could. Giving his heart to God was one thing. Living with his past was something entirely different. God couldn't erase what he'd done.

Though he didn't tell his brothers, his decision was the same. Larissa was better off without him.

Chapter Fourteen

Larissa couldn't imagine where Drew was.

She glanced out the bay window in the living room toward the garage. His truck was gone, but he'd not said a word about being out this late.

She thought about calling the Radcliffs to ask Ryan, but was too embarrassed. What kind of wife didn't know where her husband was?

This was so unlike him. He always phoned or left a note. She checked the refrigerator, the back door, the table, and a dozen other places.

In the bedroom, she looked on the dresser. Nothing.

Coco lay curled on her pillow, staring up with big eyes.

"How did you get up there, little girl?" she asked, but was too concerned about Drew to give much thought to Coco's renewed ability to jump up on the bed.

A trip down the stairs to the basement proved just as unfruitful.

"Okay, maybe he's out getting night photos."

Her few hours at Mother's had extended to late evening, as usual. She'd called a couple of times, but Drew hadn't answered. Her messages, one offering to bring home a pizza, were still on the machine. Just as the pizza was still on the kitchen counter.

Knowing Drew, he'd gone somewhere with his camera and had become enthralled with some aspect of light that normal people didn't even see. He was probably patiently waiting for the perfect shot. It wouldn't be the first time he'd gotten lost in his work.

She chalked up her disquiet to the conversation yesterday with Collin. Perhaps she'd made a mistake by not telling Drew right away. He had a right to know his brothers were looking for him.

Back in the kitchen, Larissa settled at the bar with a plate of spicy pepperoni and mushroom pizza.

She was tired to the bone. A day with Mother and one of her projects always wore her out. She'd been so tempted to blurt out how wrong they'd been about Drew. The only thing her husband had hidden was a heartbreaking past.

But it was his past and he should make the decision about how much her parents learned. They'd never shown him much sympathy, so she didn't expect that to change. If anything Mother would call him white trash and turn up her snobby nose.

With a weary sigh, she peeled a slice of pepperoni from the crust. Maybe she'd take a long bubble bath and read until Drew came home.

He'd be here soon. It was after eight. Drew loved to shoot at sunset, but that time had come and gone.

Tossing the half-eaten slice back in the box, she rolled her head from side to side, stretching the tired muscles. Then she headed for the tub.

Half an hour later, feeling relaxed and refreshed, she went into the bedroom.

Drew still wasn't home. She gnawed the side of her fingernail. Maybe she should call Ryan, just to be sure. If Drew would carry a cell phone, she wouldn't worry. What if he was driving and his vision blacked out? She shuddered at the thought. He could be in another accident.

Sitting on the side of the bed, she reached for

the phone and disturbed Coco in the process. The Yorkie struggled up from the pillow.

As Larissa reached to help the dog down onto the floor, her gaze fell on a wadded, wrinkled piece of paper.

She frowned and picked it up. "What is this?"

But she recognized Drew's scrawling cursive. "What a weird place for a note."

And then she began to read.

> *Sorry for everything. I'll file for divorce so you won't have to. Be happy. I will love you always. Drew*

Stunned, as if shot with a Taser gun, she sat there and stared at the note, reading the horrible message over and over again. With each reading, the crack in her heart expanded.

"What is he talking about? He'll always love me, but he still wants a divorce?" And he wanted her to be happy about it. What kind of sense did that make?

She thought they were working things out, that their relationship had grown stronger and better. What could have happened?

With a moan, she lay down on the bed and tried to think.

He'd promised to try. He'd even promised to consider babies. He was going to stay home more, work on the book, let his eyes heal. Why had he walked out this way?

Her mind went back over the last couple of days, searching, thinking. Finally, she settled on the only thing that made any sense at all. An assignment. His work had separated them over and over again. He must have been offered a terrific job, and knowing she would ask him to keep his promise of staying longer, had chosen the work over her again.

All his talk of staying home more, even of having a family, had been lies to keep the peace until his wounds healed.

Hard, cold reality settled in. He'd left this way because he didn't want to tell her face-to-face. He didn't want her to know where he was going.

This time he was gone forever.

And she'd never had a chance to tell him about Collin's phone call.

A tidal wave of hurt and grief welled up, threatening to send her over the edge. She cried until her eyes ached and her throat hurt. She cried until Coco's wet nose pushed at the hair over her ear, trying in vain to comfort her.

When the flood of tears finally subsided, she

crawled beneath the covers, a wad of tissues in hand, and lay staring into the darkness. The words of the note rolled over and over inside her head.

She did the only thing she knew to do. She prayed.

"He loves me, Lord. He said so. I *know* so. What happened? Where is he? I'm so confused by this. Please take care of him. Show me what to do."

After a while, unable to sleep, she sat up, clicked on the lamp, and reached for her Bible.

The phone on the bedside table jangled.

"Drew," she whispered. Heart in her throat, she lifted the receiver. "Hello."

"Larissa. Collin here. Drew's brother."

As if she could forget, especially now when she must confess that Drew was gone and the opportunity for a reunion had gone with him.

Hiding the disappointment, she said, "I'm sorry I didn't get back to you sooner."

"Drew was here tonight."

"What? Where?"

"Oklahoma City. My house. Ian's here, too. We had a nice long talk." He hesitated and she could hear him moving around. "Look, I don't know how to say this. I guess I should put Ian on the phone. He's better at talking than I am."

"Just tell me," she said, and then, to her embarrassment, her voice broke. "Drew left me, Collin. He's gone."

"I know. He told us."

"I'm sorry. I feel so foolish telling this to a complete stranger."

"We aren't strangers. We're family."

And with those simple words, the dam broke and Larissa's flood of emotions poured out. "Do you know where he's going? Did he say anything about why he left? I just don't understand any of this. I thought we had worked things out, but he wants a divorce."

"No, he doesn't. According to our brother, you won't want him now that you know about his past. Is that true?"

"Of course not. I love the man Drew has become. I don't care about the rest."

"We tried to tell him that. But Drew thinks he's not good enough for you. He made the break so you wouldn't have to."

"That's crazy."

"Yeah, well, Drew always was the crazy one. But he needs you, Larissa. Any fool could see that."

"I don't even know where he is."

"I do." He rattled off a hotel address. "I

need to tell you something else, too. Some good news for a change. Drew accepted the Lord tonight."

"Oh, Collin." She closed her eyes in gratitude. "That's wonderful."

If she wasn't so distressed she'd jump for joy. At least, Drew now had Jesus to watch over him no matter what happened.

"I agree, but he's got some cockamamie idea about heading to Indonesia."

"I don't understand this. With his vision problems, he isn't ready to be alone on assignment."

There was a subtle pause. "What vision problems?"

"Since the accident, his vision comes and goes. Sometimes everything goes black."

"Oh, man. He didn't tell us. Our poor, idiotic brother is in worse shape than we thought. And we'd already decided he was a mess. Look, Larissa, he needs you badly. Any fool could see he's dying inside. If you love him, go to him and make him understand that he's worth it. Love never fails to do what two brothers can't."

Stunned to hear Collin repeat the verse she'd clung to for months, she whispered, "What did you just say?"

"Love never fails, Larissa. Never. It may fail to do what we wanted it to at the time we expected, but love will never fail. Even if Drew is pushing you away, he's dying for you to make him stay. He has God's love, but he needs yours, too."

And through the mouth of her husband's brother, God confirmed what Larissa already suspected. She'd made mistakes, too. Her love *had* failed. It had failed because it had been a selfish love. Her own wants and needs and selfish desires had stood in the way. She'd tried to manipulate Drew into staying home, into having a baby, into being the husband she wanted. All for her own agenda.

Fearful of driving Drew away, she'd never fully trusted her marriage to the Lord. She'd been trying to control things on her own.

But no more.

Drew reclined on the brown hotel bed-spread, still fully dressed, hands stacked behind his head.

In his need to think about everything that occurred, he'd returned to the hotel over Collin's protestations. Overwhelmed, over-loaded, stunned. He couldn't think of enough adjectives to describe his emotions. This had been the strangest day of his life.

He was alternately filled with joy and then despair. His brothers, both incredibly fine men, were back in his life. He didn't even know how to begin thanking God for that miracle.

God.

He touched the ichthus at his throat. Pure, radiant light surrounded him. God had always been here, just as He'd promised. Drew only wished he hadn't taken so long to let the Lord be a real part of his life.

"Lord, I sure wish I'd known you before everything fell apart with Larissa."

Just saying her name brought heat and pressure to the back of his eyes. Angry, he slashed at them. The decision was made. No amount of talking by his brothers would change his mind. They didn't know all the facts, and when they did, they'd agree. Larissa was better off without him.

All this time, he'd prayed for God to change her. Change her mind about his work. Change her mind about having kids. All along, he was the needy one, the one in the wrong. Now that it was too late, he would give up *everything* to change his past and become the good husband Larissa deserved.

He tossed restlessly, full of donuts and milk, a jumble of thoughts.

Tomorrow he'd call Shelby, accept the book deal with instructions to look for other opportunities as well. He'd phone National Geographic himself.

Or maybe he'd wait a few days, spend some time with Collin and Ian. Man, it was good to be with them again.

Rolling to his side, he checked the standard issue alarm clock. Midnight had long since come and gone.

He flipped on the lamp, blinking in the sudden burst of illumination. His equipment bag lay on the tiny round table. In all the stress and excitement, he'd forgotten to take any pictures of his brothers. Very uncharacteristic. Tomorrow he'd rectify the oversight. Next to the bag was Ian's video.

Needing the distraction and curious about the news story that had changed his life, he rose and started toward the table.

The room faded to black.

Struck with fear, he fumbled in the darkness, bumped into a chair, scraped it back and sat.

He waited, hoping, praying the darkness would dissipate as usual.

Stress brought this on. He was sure of it. He took slow, deep breaths, fighting for calm. He could control his mind. Hadn't the doctors said so?

Fingertips pressed to his eyelids, he concentrated on turning the inner lights back on.

What would he do if that didn't happen?

The air-conditioning snicked into action, and cool, slightly musty air whooshed through the room.

Nothing wrong with the rest of his senses.

Maybe a good night's sleep would restore the vision. No doubt he was overtired and stressed to the max.

Moving around in the unfamiliar room was tricky, but he felt his way to the bed. Flickers of light flashed behind his eyes.

He shook his head. Once. Twice.

The flickers came again, brighter, longer.

"Come on. Come on."

In the next instant, he realized what he'd forgotten. He wasn't alone anymore. He had Someone to help him through life's darkest places. Carefully, he slipped to his knees beside the bed.

"Lord, I don't know the right way to ask You for things. But the way I figure it, You created eyes in the first place, so if You would please, I need my sight back. I'm a photographer. You probably know that."

Then an overwhelming sense of regret and remorse took hold of him. He began to pray anew, for his messed-up life, for Larissa, for the terrible sin he'd committed all those years ago.

Though he knew next to nothing of prayer, he figured God understood anyway. The words poured out for a long time. How long he couldn't say. He couldn't see the clock.

Finally, he murmured, "Well, that's all, I guess. Thanks for listening."

He opened his eyes, disappointed to still be in the dark. And then a powerful realization swelled inside him. He might be physically blind forever, but spiritual darkness was a choice. He would never be completely free of the dark past until he faced it head-on. Tonight he'd done that in part by meeting with his brothers. But the deeper issue still hung over him like a noose.

Memories of that terrible night rolled through him. Memories that had shaped his entire life and crippled him in a way the roadside bomb never could.

Smoking in the attic. Falling asleep, only to

awaken to screams. The flames shooting high into the night sky, consuming everything and everyone.

For years, he'd blocked the visions, but now he let them come. He saw the dying faces. Heard the moans and screams. Tasted the acrid smoke that had left him hoarse for days.

Sweat popped out over his body. But he watched the movie inside his head.

He'd committed this atrocity. He'd killed those boys with his careless disregard of authority.

It was time to stand up and face the consequences of his actions. No more running. No more hiding. He was a man now, not a scared runaway with nowhere to turn.

First thing in the morning he'd call the Oklahoma City police department and turn himself in. Not to Collin. That was too heavy a burden to place on his older brother. The only person he would lean on was himself—and God.

Unless his vision cleared, the cops would have to come for him. He could deal with that.

Blood pounding against his temples, both scared and relieved, he rested back on the pillow to await the morning.

Some time later, he heard footsteps in the hallway. Then someone tapped softly at the door.

He sat upright, listening hard.

A visitor in the middle of the night? House-keeping? A guest gone astray? Burglars?

"Go away," he called. "The room is occupied."

"Drew. Honey."

His heart slammed against his rib cage. His beautiful wife, the love of his life stood outside in the hallway.

Not knowing what else to do, he got up and felt his way to the door. "Go home, Larissa."

If she saw him now, blind and scared, she'd force him back to Tulsa. He couldn't do that to her.

"Open the door, Drew. I'll stand out here all night if you don't." When he didn't respond, she pecked on the door again. "It's a long drive up here. I'm really tired. Please let me in."

The woman didn't play fair. He'd let her in, but he would not let her stay.

He felt for the security lock, struggling to work the chain through the hole.

"Drew?"

Frustrated, he bit out, "One minute."

Was this what he had to look forward to?

As metal rattled against metal, the chain fell away and he reached for the deadbolt, finally opening the heavy door.

And there she stood, as clear as the morning sun.

His mouth must have gaped. He could see her. For a second, he sagged, mentally screaming thank-you to the God of the universe.

Larissa never needed to know what he'd just gone through.

As soon as he had his wits about him, he said, "What are you doing here?"

She pushed inside. "Don't play tough guy with me. I know what you're trying to do."

"Yeah?" He turned his back to her. If he was rude, maybe she would leave before he collapsed at her feet and cried like a baby. "I'm trying to get some sleep."

"Then why was the light on?"

He rubbed a hand over his eyes, refusing to go there.

"Why are you here, Larissa? What do you want?" He stared at a picture on the wall, grateful to see it.

Larissa swept around in front of him, blocking the sight. He couldn't complain. She was far more beautiful than the abstract slash of blues and greens. "I love you, and I won't let you go."

"You don't have a choice. I'm leaving. Again. Just like always. Nothing's changed."

"Liar," she said softly, but tears gathered in the corners of her violet eyes and nearly brought him to his knees. "I talked to Collin. He told me about your past. Your childhood. How hard it was."

Bitter gall rose in his throat. She knew too much. "Collin's got a big mouth."

"I'm thankful, Drew. At last I can understand what makes you do the things you do. All this time I thought you loved your cameras and your travel more than me. But now I know better."

She'd just arrived and already he was losing ground. "Go home, Larissa."

But his gentle wife had a relentless side. She shook her head, gold hoops peeking through long, silky hair. "You run because you're afraid."

"I'm a disaster photographer. I'm not afraid of anything."

"Yes, you are. You're afraid of me. Afraid to let someone love you. Afraid of being rejected again. Afraid to trust. So you run."

The issue was far more complicated than she could know. He wasn't running anymore. But he wasn't about to saddle the woman he loved with a convict. Knowing Larissa she would stand by her man until the bitter end. He could live with his punishment. He couldn't live with knowing he'd ruined her life.

"A bunch of psychobabble nonsense."

"Really?" Head to one side, she perched hands on her hips. "Then why did you hide your past from me? Why did you change your name and create an entirely new identity?"

Humiliation added fuel to his pretend anger. "Collin does have a big mouth."

"Collin didn't tell me. My father did."

"Your father?"

"He had you investigated." When he opened his mouth to give his opinion of that little invasion of privacy, she held up a palm. "Hear me out. I've already said all the things you're thinking. I told my parents, essentially, to stay out of our relationship because I know the real you. An investigation did not change my feelings."

Jaw tight, he said, "It should have."

"The investigation didn't. But the Lord did."

The admission stabbed him through the heart. So she'd finally come to her senses. Good. He just wished it didn't hurt so much.

Then she shocked him by saying, "I need your forgiveness, Drew. The Lord showed me how selfish I've been in our marriage. I wanted everything my way. I wanted to force you into the mold of my making. I've tried to change you, to make you do things my way. Instead of easing your fear and distrust, I added to it."

Oh, man. His walls began to crumble.

"You don't know what you're talking about," he growled.

"Your past makes you who you are, Drew. And I love the man you've become. You're incredible."

"I'm a loser. If you're smart you'll be the one who runs—as fast as you can away from me."

She shook her head and moved closer. Her sweet perfume wafted over him like a summer breeze. He stepped back.

"Listen to me, Drew. I know you better than you know yourself. You took a terrible childhood and turned it into a successful life."

"Yeah, right. Name one good thing I've ever done."

"I can name dozens. You give children in dire situations a voice with your pictures. You mentored a troubled kid that no one else could stand having around." Love glimmered in the big violet eyes. "You slept on the floor with my dog because I was so worried about her."

He sniffed. "Big deal."

She touched his arm. Though he should shake her off, he couldn't. Her touch was like a salve to an open wound. "You have my heart,

Drew. If you leave, you take it with you. No matter what happens, I'll still love you. Love, God's kind of love, never fails. Never."

He heard the hope in her words, saw it in her eyes. Refusing her was the hardest thing he'd ever had to do.

Like a battered prize fighter rising for one last round, he managed to say, "There are things you don't know. Things that will make you hate me. I can't go back to Tulsa because—" Emotion clogged the back of his throat. He had to say the words and drive her away. "Tomorrow morning I'm going to jail."

She blinked. Once. Twice. Dear Lord, he loved her.

"What are you talking about?" she whispered, and the trembling voice tore him up.

"A long time ago, before I became Drew Michaels, I did something terrible." He sucked in a gulp of stale hotel air. He'd tell her and then send her home. "It's time I faced the consequences."

"I don't understand."

"Well here it is. I killed some people."

She gasped, hand pressed to her lips. "You did not."

"People thought I died in a house fire." He grabbed both her arms and pulled her close, grim and determined. "I didn't die, but lots of others did. And it was my fault. I killed those kids."

He expected her to jerk away in revulsion, but she didn't. His amazing, incredible wife walked straight into his chest and wrapped her arms around him. He stood there, arms at his side, lost in the beauty of her love.

"Didn't you hear me?" he choked out, desperate now.

She only shook her head, then began to rock him back and forth, back and forth, holding him in a grip that refused to let go.

"Oh, my Drew," she murmured. "Let me hold you. Let me love the little boy who needed someone, and no one was there. Let me be here for you now. And forever."

Drew squeezed his eyes tight against the piercing sweet emotion. Her tears dampened his shirt, adding to his guilt.

"Listen to me," he pled. "I killed those kids. I caused that fire."

She leaned back, face wet with tears, still refusing to release him. "Tell me everything. Everything."

"If I do, will you go? Will you walk away and never look back? Will you start again and pretend you never knew me?"

"No." She touched the ichthus at his throat. "Jesus will never leave you nor forsake you. I won't either."

"Oh, God," he moaned, looking up at the ceiling. "Please make her see."

His ugly sin hung in the air between them. Clinging to one last chance to set her free, he tugged her down to the side of the bed.

Then he told her everything.

"You already know I was a wild teenager. Angry. Bucking authority. There wasn't much I wouldn't or didn't do." He sucked in a shuddering breath. "Another kid and I hid cigarettes in the attic. After the house parents were asleep, we'd sneak up there and smoke. We thought we were cool."

He shook his head, so sorry for the pain and sorrow he'd caused. "We were so stupid."

Her hand rubbed up and down his arm, soothing. "What happened?"

"I fell asleep. The next thing I knew people were screaming and running, and the house was full of smoke." Vivid memories flashed in his head, cruel but useful. "I jumped out the window and ran. Too scared to come back and face the music, I hid out. The next morning, the paper said everyone died. Including me. I knew if I went back, I'd end up in some institution for the emotionally disturbed or worse, in prison. So I let Drew Grace die in that fire along with everyone else."

"Oh, Drew." Larissa fell against him. He caught her in his arms and held on, letting some of his shame flow out. Several silent moments ticked by while his wife embraced him for the last time.

Suddenly, Larissa sat bolt upright and gripped his arms. "Wait a minute. Wait just a minute." She gave him a little shake. "Drew, listen to me. I don't think you caused that fire."

Hope died hard in this lady. "Well, think again. I was there."

"Where? Tell me again exactly where you were inside that house."

For whatever good it would do, he humored her. "In the attic. The house mother was—" his mouth quirked "—chubby. She couldn't climb the ladder. It was the perfect hiding place, filled with old boxes and books and used furniture. Add cigarettes and matches and you have a recipe for disaster."

Her eyes danced with an excitement he couldn't comprehend. "That's it then. Drew, you didn't cause that tragedy. The fire started in the kitchen."

A flicker of hope trembled in his chest. "How could you possibly know that?"

"The TV report. Collin talked about a kitchen fire. Not an attic fire."

Could it be true? "Are you sure?"

"I recorded the segment. Let's go home and watch it."

"No need." He got up and went to the table, hoisting the videotape. "Ian gave me a copy. I rented a VCR downstairs but hadn't gotten around to watching."

Being blind put a damper on watching TV. More hopeful than he'd been in years, he slid the tape into the machine. His hands, so steady with a camera, trembled.

Five minutes later he was a free man.

He looked at his wife. Her face glowed with happiness.

"You didn't cause that fire," she said in wonder.

"I didn't kill those kids," he whispered, hardly able to take it in. All these years of self-loathing and fear, all the lies and hiding.

"I'm free." Tears prickled the back of his eyes, but these were tears of release and happiness. "I'm free."

He pulled her into his arms, this time as a man with the right to love a good woman. Though he'd never deserve her loyalty and love, he could now accept it. And give the same in return.

"I love you, Larissa," he murmured against her hair. "I'm sorry for all the times I've hurt you."

"No more talk of divorce?" she murmured, her soft breath tickling his ear.

"I never wanted a divorce. It was a lie concocted to scare you away. Will you forgive me?"

"If you'll forgive me, too, and promise never to keep secrets again."

There in the tiny hotel room, he pulled her to her feet. They held hands, facing one another as they had when they'd exchanged wedding vows.

"No more secrets." Later, he'd share the vision problems. Right now, he wanted to bask in the moment of release and freedom. "When problems arise, we'll talk them out."

"If you want to travel with your job, I won't whine. Military wives handle the separations. So can I."

"I'll be home more. I want to be."

"I won't nag about a family until you're ready."

Nearing overload, he swallowed the lump of emotion. "I think I am."

"What?"

He loved putting the joy in her eyes. "You. Me. A little rug rat or two. Sounds pretty good."

"I love you so much."

"The feeling, Mrs. Michaels, is mutual."

They stared into one another's eyes for several long, sweet, healing seconds. And then, in one movement, Drew grabbed Larissa around the waist and hoisted her high. He whirled her round and round until they both were laughing with joy and relief.

When the euphoria subsided, he set her on her feet and said, "Ready to go home?"

Her smile was beautiful.

"Right after you kiss me."

Feeling strong and confident and a little cocky, he grinned. "I think I can handle that."

And he did.

Epilogue

On a quiet side street in Oklahoma City, on a typical Saturday in July, a not-so-typical celebration occurred.

Drew, Collin and Ian, the three Grace brothers were together again as a family. Only this time, the family had increased so much Drew could hardly take it in. In fact, he'd already taken four rolls of film and was working on a fifth.

He breathed a lungful of oregano-scented air. The smell was pure contentment, a new and unexpected bonus of finding his brothers and a life in Christ.

Next to him at the long, food-laden table was Larissa, the woman who had never given up even when leaving would have been more sensible and much easier. He squeezed her hand and was rewarded with her gentle smile.

"Good, huh?" she murmured.

"Better than good."

Drew gazed around the big, crowded dining room. His brothers sat across the table with their own ladies.

Rounding out the group was the Carano family along with Ian's feisty adoptive mother, Margot Carpenter. The lady, who'd traveled with Ian and Gretchen from Louisiana, was a blend of genteel Southern belle and solid steel. Her devotion to Ian—and the woman he'd chosen as his wife—was evident. And what could he say about the exuberant Carano family? They were as warm as the Oklahoma summer.

Though he was a bit overwhelmed, Drew liked them all.

The Carano house was older, comfortable, a place that welcomed visitors like family. A place that embraced the noise and mess of kids. A place where love was as abundant as pastries, and every bit as sweet.

This was the kind of family life the Grace brothers had only dreamed about. But the Lord always knew where the long, broken road would lead.

Drew had never imagined Collin, the tough loner, as part of a huge Italian family either. But here he was all smiles and jokes with his fiancée's gaggle of brothers, Nic, Adam, and Gabe who were giving him a hard time about marrying their sister.

All afternoon, the women had perused bridal magazines and made to-do lists in preparation for the double wedding of Ian to Gretchen and Collin to Mia. The date was set for Christmas, a fitting time, Drew thought, for a glorious celebration of love.

For now, the meal was essentially over, but the dining table seemed the perfect spot for conversation. So the adults remained, talking, sipping tea, munching Mama Carano's chocolate biscotti.

Mia, who never seemed to stop talking or waving her expressive hands somehow managed to wave everyone to silence.

"I asked Ian to bring his saxophone for a special reason. By the grace of God, the Grace brothers are all back together again. And not only have they found each other, they've found us!" Her wide mouth stretched in a happy grin as everyone chuckled. "I think there is something wonderfully significant about all that grace. So I've asked Ian to play a special song."

She nodded toward his baby brother who was just returning from the other room with his saxophone in hand. Drew hadn't even known his brother was a musician. He supposed they'd be learning things about each other for a long time to come.

Ian lifted the gleaming instrument and music flowed out like rough honey. Almost immediately, the listeners picked up the melody, first in low, murmuring voices, but soon the lyrics swelled in thanksgiving and wonder.

"Amazing grace, how sweet the sound that saved a wretch like me. I once was lost but now I'm found. Was blind but now I see…"

Drew had never given the song much thought before, but now he listened with every cell in his body. Whoever had written the words had lived them. So had he. He'd been blind, spiritually and emotionally, but God had turned on the lights. The light to a relationship with the Lord and to a strong marriage. And even if the light of his vision was forever extinguished, the other two would shine bright enough to sustain him.

When the last notes died away, he pulled his wife against his side and nuzzled her hair.

"I love you," he whispered. "And I thank God

every day for the amazing grace that brought us to this point."

Her radiant smile washed over him. "Me, too."

"Everything would be perfect if…"

"Your vision?" She frowned, the action drawing her perfect eyebrows together in a way that made him want to smooth a finger over them. He never wanted Larissa to frown or cry or be sad again.

"No. Not even that." His agent had sold the book proposal for a lot of money with an option for more. And there was talk of him teaching a photography class in Tulsa. "I hope my vision is back for good, but if not—" he shrugged, amazed to really believe his words "—we'll be okay. God will take care of us."

"Yes. I believe that with all my heart. But why did you say everything would be perfect *if?*"

"Your parents. You love them. They hate me. I'm sorry about that." More sorry than he could ever say. "I know how important family is, especially now. I don't want to take yours from you. I'd do about anything to mend fences with them."

A sweet secret smile tipped his wife's full, lush mouth. "I think you already have."

He tilted his head, puzzled.

Larissa went on, her violet eyes glowing. "I have a secret that may do the trick."

He offered a mock scowl. "We promised not to keep secrets, remember?"

"That's why I'm about to reveal all." Around them, the assembled group chattered and laughed, paying them no mind. Larissa leaned in to whisper, "Mother and Dad have wanted grandchildren for a long time."

The air above Drew buzzed with energy and sucked his breath away. Was she saying what he thought she was saying? "Are you—?"

His heart beat so hard, he thought he'd have a heart attack. And it wasn't caused by overindulging on Mama Carano's lasagna.

"I mean, Daddy Drew, you and I are going to have a baby."

Drew had expected to be scared, but he wasn't. Not at all. He was ecstatic. Adrenaline rushed to his head. Without stopping to remember where they were, he cried, "Yes!" and bolted from the chair.

The clatter of forks died away. A dozen pairs of eyes stared in astonishment. Drew didn't care. He tenderly pulled his beautiful, pregnant wife up into his arms and kissed her.

A half-dozen catcalls circled the room.

When the kiss ended, Drew draped an arm around Larissa and turned to blurt, "We're having a baby."

The noise started up again. This time congratulations and hugs were in order. Collin and Ian pounded his back until he feared they'd rebreak his ribs. Larissa glowed as the women huddled around to ask due dates and discuss the mysteries of childbirth.

And as the circle of family surrounded him, Drew lifted a silent prayer of thanksgiving to Heaven. For his wife, the new extended family, the tiny blend of himself and Larissa that would join them early next year. And of course, for his brothers.

As Gretchen's news report so beautifully phrased it, he, Ian and Collin were separated as boys, but reunited as men. But the bond that had brought them together again was more than a bond of blood. It was a bond of family. A bond of love.

A gift of God.

Larissa turned to him with one of her smiles.

Yes, a gift of God. And he would never, ever again take that gift for granted.

* * * * *

Dear Reader,

Thank you for choosing *The Heart of Grace,* the final book in The Brothers' Bond trilogy. I hope you have enjoyed reading about the Grace brothers as much as I have enjoyed writing about them. I must confess to a mix of joy and sadness in bringing their stories to a close. Somewhere out there are three little boys who first inspired this series. I hope and pray that they, too, have found a happy ending.

As always I enjoy hearing from readers and value their thoughts on my stories. You may contact me at www.lindagoodnight.com or at Linda Goodnight, c/o Steeple Hill Books, 233 Broadway, Suite 1001, New York, NY 10279.

God bless the needy children of the world. And God bless you, as well.

Linda Goodnight

QUESTIONS FOR DISCUSSION

1. Drew's difficult past taints every aspect of his present. What does the Bible teach us about handling our past problems?

2. Can a person really ever overcome a dysfunctional childhood? How?

3. After Drew accepts the Lord, he wants to take responsibility for the fire. God says our sins, once forgiven, are washed away in a sea of forgetfulness never more to be remembered by Him. Should the new Christian simply forget the past? Or should he, as Drew wanted to do, pay restitution for previous wrongs?

4. Larissa believes that a Christian can never divorce. Is this true? Are there scriptural guidelines for divorce?

5. If Drew had divorced Larissa against her wishes, would remarriage be a sin for her?

6. Do you think God ever causes something bad to happen, such as an accident or an illness to bring a person closer to Him?

7. Why does Drew never attempt to find his brothers?

8. Larissa clings to the verse, "Love never fails." Is this true? What kind of love is implied here? Is all love the same?

9. Is orphan ministry only for a few? Or is every believer called to take care of the widows and orphans? What scripture confirms your stance? Does this stance also apply to social orphans like Drew and his brothers?